W9-BVI-742

"I Can't Be With You. You Lied. And I'm Through With Liars. You Have To Understand That. We'll Get A Divorce. Go Our Separate Ways."

"It's not that simple. Other people are involved."

"You can't make me come back to you, Connor."

"Oh, yes I can, sweetheart…. Money buys a lot of what passes for justice in this country. I've got money—lots of it. You don't. I can afford top-notch legal talent. You can't."

"I hate you. I'll hate you forever."

"But you're a survivor, so that won't stop you from coming home with me and living with me as my wife now that you see how it's to your advantage, now will it?" He pushed back his Stetson. "Because if you do that, sweetheart—and only if you do that—I'll keep all your dirty little secrets."

Dear Reader,

Some books are harder to write than others. Who knows why?

For a long time I've felt I've been living in a three-ring circus, and all the acts in every ring are out of control. Several tragedies and many crises occurred while I was writing this novel.

They say writers harvest their worst moments. Hopefully, I will have a run of good luck for a while, as I have plenty of material for years to come.

This book is the last in my four-book GOLDEN SPURS series. Connor Storm has been paid to find the ranch's long-missing heiress, Becky. Their relationship gets off to a rocky start when he falls in love, but doesn't tell her who he is or who she is, and then marries her. When she discovers part of the truth, she thinks she can never trust such a man and flees.

When he later learns they have a little girl, who looks like him, he goes after them and brings them home. This time he will do whatever it takes to make the relationship work.

Surely, no heroine has ever needed a happily-ever-after ending more than Becky, although it takes Connor a while to make her realize it.

Enjoy,

Ann Major

ANN MAJOR

THE BRIDE HUNTER

Silhouette® Desire

Published by Silhouette Books

America's Publisher of Contemporary Romance

If you purchased this book without a cover you should be aware that this book is stolen property. It was reported as "unsold and destroyed" to the publisher, and neither the author nor the publisher has received any payment for this "stripped book."

SILHOUETTE BOOKS

PLEASE RECYCLE
THIS PRODUCT IS RECYCLABLE

Recycling programs
for this product may
not exist in your area.

ISBN-13: 978-0-373-76945-2

THE BRIDE HUNTER

Copyright © 2009 by Ann Major

All rights reserved. Except for use in any review, the reproduction or utilization of this work in whole or in part in any form by any electronic, mechanical or other means, now known or hereafter invented, including xerography, photocopying and recording, or in any information storage or retrieval system, is forbidden without the written permission of the editorial office, Silhouette Books, 233 Broadway, New York, NY 10279 U.S.A.

This is a work of fiction. Names, characters, places and incidents are either the product of the author's imagination or are used fictitiously, and any resemblance to actual persons, living or dead, business establishments, events or locales is entirely coincidental.

This edition published by arrangement with Harlequin Books S.A.

® and TM are trademarks of Harlequin Books S.A., used under license. Trademarks indicated with ® are registered in the United States Patent and Trademark Office, the Canadian Trade Marks Office and in other countries.

Visit Silhouette Books at www.eHarlequin.com

Printed in U.S.A.

Recent books by Ann Major

Silhouette Desire

Midnight Fantasy #1304
Cowboy Fantasy #1375
A Cowboy & a Gentleman #1477
Shameless #1513
The Bride Tamer #1586
The Amalfi Bride #1784
Sold into Marriage #1832
Mistress for a Month #1869
*The Throw-Away Bride #1912
*The Bride Hunter #1945

MIRA Books

The Girl with the Golden Spurs
The Girl with the Golden Gun
The Secret Lives of Doctors' Wives

*Golden Spurs

ANN MAJOR

lives in Texas with her husband of many years and is the mother of three grown children. She has a master's degree from Texas A&M at Kingsville, Texas, and is a former English teacher. She is a founding board member of the Romance Writers of America and a frequent speaker at writers' groups.

Ann loves to write; she considers her ability to do so a gift. Her hobbies include hiking in the mountains, sailing, ocean kayaking, traveling and playing the piano. But most of all she enjoys her family. Visit her Web site at www.annmajor.com.

This book is for Diana Fasano Gafford, my dearest girlfriend for more than forty years, whom I lost to an unexpected illness while writing this novel.

Diana loved romance novels and inspired me to start writing them. She had all my books lined up on her top bookshelf and always read them as soon as they hit the stands.

She was a teacher, and she inspired many students. She believed in love and romance. She brightened every day that she was here on earth, and I've missed her every day that she's been gone.

This book is for you, Diana.

That said, I owe a special thanks to my editor, Krista Stroever, for all her hard work in helping me reshape the final draft.

One

His large body humming with tension, Connor Storm fixed on his prey. The woman, who went by the alias Anna Barton, had eluded his top investigator. Now she was sipping the coffee she'd just bought at the kiosk behind her. Connor was trying to keep out of her line of vision by standing behind a pillar while they both waited for their plane to be called.

Her face was fine boned, her shiny hair dark blond and shoulder length. He liked long hair. He didn't like the fact that he was suddenly imagining his big hand grasping her thick mane and pulling her closer.

Damn. First time since Linda he'd thought like this about a woman. He must be coming back to the land of the living.

This is a job. For Leo. You owe your big brother. There are a lot of other fish in the sea. Yada, yada.

At five foot seven, his target was slim and athletic—and very pretty.

Don't think about very pretty.

Their plane was an hour late due to bad weather. He glanced impatiently at his watch and out the large window again. The snow had let up. He could see the end of the runway now.

A woman's voice came over a loudspeaker and announced their plane would be boarding at Gate 10 instead of Gate 14. The crowd in the Gate 14 waiting area stood up and began gathering briefcases and laptops. Anna Barton jumped away from the kiosk as fast as a bird taking flight and rushed toward their gate.

His cue to pursue and capture.

Planting his Stetson firmly on his blond head, Connor Storm charged after her, his boot heels ringing so loudly on the airport terminal floor that she whirled, her hazel eyes wide with alarm.

Perhaps on the lookout for the creepy boyfriend who'd been stalking her?

"Hey, miss! You'll need this if you want to board that flight anytime soon!" he yelled.

When the elusive woman he'd been paid so much to find stopped, Connor froze midstride.

Distrust was written all over her. Her gaze traveled the length of him before flitting away. Connor was suddenly glad he'd taken Sam Guerra off this assignment and come himself.

Her tall, slender body fairly shook with tension. Clearly

she still didn't trust strangers, especially if they were broad-shouldered men who could easily overpower her. Her boyfriend, Dwight Crawford, must have been an even worse nutcase than his P.I.'s reports had indicated.

Connor tipped his Stetson back and attempted one of his easy smiles.

She stiffened.

He broadened his grin. Then he flapped the boarding pass he'd removed from her purse while she'd been too busy counting change to buy coffee.

"I was behind you in line when you dropped this," he lied, feeling only a slight pang of guilt at his easy falsehood.

He was a private investigator. P.I.s had to make stuff up in the line of duty, right? They had a nice word for it, too. *Pretext,* they called it.

Her face remained pinched, her eyes wary. He'd had his guy on her tail for a while. Every time he had gotten close, she'd run, changing her identity.

Her creamy skin was pale and looked so soft, Connor wanted to touch it. Damn, the pretty factor was becoming a problem.

This was a job. For Leo, he reminded himself.

Her big, slanting eyes seemed so vulnerable and scared, he had half a mind to track the boyfriend down and teach him a lesson. A woman who'd gone through what she had as a child didn't deserve some slimeball like Crawford scaring her again.

She lifted her nose. She was slim and statuesque. She had class. With her heritage, he'd expected no less. In

Texas, anybody connected to the Golden Spurs ranching empire was royalty.

His job was to take her home. Period.

Funny, how she wore her hair down just like Abby did. He'd read separated twins did stuff like that. Still, the startlingly similar hairdo made her look so exactly like his brother Leo's wife, Connor drew in a sharp breath. Not that he should have been surprised at the resemblance—after all, she was Abby's long-lost kidnapped twin.

What was strange was his powerful reaction to her. Hell, he'd never felt blistering heat when staring into his sister-in-law's eyes.

"Becky," he whispered, gut-sure he'd found the Golden Spurs heiress.

At the name, Anna shivered. Her big, haunted eyes widened.

"Becky? I don't know who you're looking for, mister," she said, "but it's not me."

"Sorry," he said. "Right. For a second you looked like somebody I know."

Her patrician nose tilted higher.

"You're Anna Barton, and you're not going anywhere without your boarding pass."

Maybe she wasn't listening, because she turned and marched quickly toward their gate.

"Anna Barton!" he yelled after her.

She speeded up, so he sprinted, catching her in two long strides.

"Anna! Anna Barton!" When she still didn't stop, he grabbed her arm, maybe a little too forcefully, because when he spun her around, she toppled straight into him, her paper coffee cup flying out of her hand.

"Ohhhh," she ground out. "Let me go!"

Other passengers turned to stare. Fortunately, no security guards were nearby.

"Sorry about that," he said, his voice muffled against her hair. His grip loosened. "I owe you a cup of coffee."

In those seconds that he held her, he felt the heat of her slim body squirming against his own, smelled the floral scent of her perfume and the soapier, sweeter fragrance of her shampoo. Her hair felt like silk against his mouth. The urge to coil a length of it around his fist and pull her even closer was becoming way too strong.

A twist of his head brought his lips mere inches from hers. When he found himself staring down at her lips, his heart raced.

"You are Anna Barton?" he growled huskily, holding up her boarding pass.

Reading her name, her wide eyes accused him. Then she snapped it out of his fingers and shoved it into her purse. "Why did you call me Becky a while ago?"

"A thank-you would be nice."

"I asked you a question," she said.

"Like I said, you…er…look like someone I used to know."

"Well, I'm not her. I've never seen you before in my life, and I'm not in the habit of making friends with strange men in airports—so, would you please let me go…and leave me alone."

It wasn't a question.

"Sorry. Sure. Just trying to help."

Yeah, right.

Her eyes were blazing now, and a rosy flush lit her cheeks. The longer he held her, the hotter her body felt against his, so hot he wanted to pull her even closer, to taste her, to kiss those lips that looked so moist and inviting.

Her gaze was fixed on his mouth, too. She seemed to be holding her breath.

With a sigh of what sounded like longing, she tore her gaze from his mouth and shoved at his broad chest.

Reluctantly, he let her go and held his hands up in mock surrender.

She straightened her long sleeves and smoothed her hair. Then with a parting scowl, she left for the gate.

Great hips. Great swing to her walk. But bouncy, too.

This is a job.

He wished he hadn't grabbed her because he needed her trust, to convince her to come back to Texas with him.

So what would it take now to get her to Houston?

Whatever it was, he'd do it. Anna Barton was Leo's sister-in-law. Leo's wife was heartbroken about the role she'd played in her twin's kidnapping when they'd been kids. She believed Leo could and would find out what had happened to her missing sister. As a result, Leo had turned to Connor and had put the same kind of pressure on him.

"Find her. For me. For Abby. She'll never rest easy if you don't," Leo had said. "It's like a piece of her is missing."

Leo had raised Connor after their mother had died. Connor owed Leo everything.

This wasn't a job.

This was family. And nothing mattered more.

* * *

The stewardess announced that the plane was full and asked passengers to take the first available seat.

"Hello," Connor said, smiling broadly down at Anna. She was pretending to be absorbed in a SkyMall catalog. "Mind if I take the aisle seat beside you?"

Without looking up, she frowned. Silently, she scooped her purse of the seat and shoved it under the seat in front of her.

He took his time placing his Stetson in the overhead bin before he sat down. He was so large, or the seat was so small, his shoulder brushed against hers, and once again he felt her body heat, which was surprisingly high voltage, since the place felt like an icebox. Hell, she all but shot off sparks every time he touched her.

"Who are you shopping for so diligently?" he asked.

Ignoring him, she flipped a page.

"You one of those people who hates to talk on a flight?"

She flipped another page, this one more noisily than the last.

"You must be like me. Usually, I have a thirty-minute rule when I sit by someone I don't know on an airplane. I never start up a conversation until thirty minutes before we're supposed to land. That way you don't get trapped."

Still, she didn't say anything. He thought maybe he should stop pestering her. Then he saw her lips twitch at the corners.

"Do you have that rule?" he whispered, bending so his breath stirred a tendril of hair against her temple.

She sighed, which made him think maybe he was having some luck after all.

"Who dreams up all those crazy things in catalogs… I

mean to tempt weak consumers like me who suddenly find themselves longing for a self-cleaning kitty litter box when I don't even have a cat."

"You could stick to your rule and read your own catalog, you know," she said.

Finally. She'd actually said something.

She pointed to the seat in front of him. "There's one in every seat pocket."

"It's way more fun reading yours."

"I can't imagine why," she said, blushing.

"Can't you?"

When she looked up into his eyes, he suddenly felt too warm to wear his sheepskin jacket, so he shrugged out of it. He couldn't believe it when her slim fingers tugged his sleeves down for him, and just that light touch was a tease.

Then she jerked her hand away.

"Thanks," he muttered in a tight, low tone.

"No problem," she said, so sweetly he wondered if she realized she was getting under his skin, too.

The pretty factor coupled with the voltage factor was a growing problem. If only he had let Leo set him up with that hot secretary he'd told him about last week…

When her attention turned back to her catalog again, he couldn't let it go.

"My wife died," he blurted, resenting this woman's appeal. He hadn't intended to say that. Linda was none of this woman's business.

Anna's face softened.

"A couple of years ago," he continued, his voice raw now.

"I'm sorry." Her eyes glowed with sympathy.

"I haven't dated since," he muttered.

The catalog slipped through her fingers to her lap. Her pretty eyes focused on him, drew him.

"I guess I'm rusty when it comes to talking to women."

"It's not just you," she whispered. "I don't date. Or talk to men, either. Especially strangers. You should have sat by someone else."

"Why don't you talk…to men?"

"I've made a lot of wrong choices, so I've decided to avoid that whole scene for a while."

"And you think I'm the wrong type?"

"It's nothing personal. It's just that I'm just not a good judge of character."

"Okay, change of subject. Why are you going to Vegas?"

Her face darkened. "I don't know why I'm telling you this. Maybe it's because you gave me back my boarding pass. Most people wouldn't even have bothered. You've got to be halfway decent."

Right. His top man had been hunting her for several months and had driven her from her job.

"The last man I dated didn't want to break up. He wouldn't leave me alone. He called. He came by my apartment, sometimes late at night. Finally, I had to move. When he showed up a few months later at the office in St. Louis, where I'd relocated to get away from him, I moved to New Mexico. I used to be a secretary, but I've been working in a school for traumatized children in Santa Fe this past year. I really loved it. For the first time, my job didn't seem like a job. Then my boss started getting calls from a private detective asking about me. And the detective showed up, looking for me. I was afraid of my boyfriend—"

Connor tensed. "How did you know this P.I. was working for your boyfriend?" he asked, careful to make his tone neutral.

"Who else would have an interest in tracking me?"

Right. Who else? Connor ignored his guilt. "So you're running again? To Vegas? Why Vegas?"

"New job. I'm going to be a housekeeping supervisor at one of the biggest hotels on the strip."

"You went from a school you loved to housekeeping in a hotel?"

"I had to find something fast. It was hard to leave that school—I'd made a breakthrough with a little boy named Daniel." As her voice trailed off wistfully, her eyes grew tender. "His family had died, you see. He was all alone. Somehow I understood him. Maybe I'd like to teach."

"So, why don't you?"

"It must be nice to believe anything's possible. Maybe someday." She turned and stared out at the clouds. "I'd have to go to college."

After that, it grew easier to talk to her. He told her about being a marine in Afghanistan, about Linda dying in the accident not long after he'd come home, about the baby he hadn't known Linda was carrying. He hadn't told anybody except Leo about his child dying.

Anna listened, her eyes huge now, and it began to worry him that their relationship felt so personal.

He didn't know how much she remembered about her childhood, about what had happened to her. But maybe since she'd had all her ties cut when she was so young, she understood what it was like to lose everything the way he did.

Bringing her back to Texas was supposed to be a job.

Enough sharing. Connor needed to cut to the chase, figure out a way to make Anna come back to Texas with him. But how? What if she bolted and went underground again?

"Are you a cowboy?" she asked.

Okay. Was this his opportunity to get down to business? He stared at his watch. They'd be landing soon. He was running out of time.

"What makes you ask?"

"The hat. The boots. Your drawl."

"I don't have a drawl."

She laughed. Her face lit up, and that made her prettier than ever. He felt another jolt.

"You most certainly do," she teased, her eyes sparkling now. "So, why the cowboy hat?"

He hesitated, feeling drawn, yet wanting to stop the charade. "I own a ranch near Austin with my older brother. Leo."

The truth, but not the whole truth. "We run some cattle," he continued. "We grew up on a ranch in west Texas. Cows and horses and wide-open spaces are in our blood. Leo manages the Golden Spurs, which is one of the biggest ranches in Texas."

They kept talking even after the plane had landed. He hurried down the jetway with Anna while trying to think up a ruse to maintain their fledgling friendship. He had to buy more time.

When they were in the terminal, she turned and smiled. "Well…it was nice talking to you."

Clearly this was goodbye.

He stared at her, unable to think because of the rattle of coins and the flash of lights from the nearby slot machines.

Slot machines.

"I'm feeling lucky." He dug in his pocket. "Will you put a dollar in a machine for me?"

"Can't you do it yourself?"

"Sure. But call it a hunch."

Her bright eyes met his again and clung in one of those endless, wordless moments. He drew a swift, ragged breath. Why did he feel like he was losing pieces of himself every time she looked at him like that? Her mouth trembled. Her eyes sparkled.

He wanted to hold her, to kiss her. Instead, he caught her palm and slapped a shiny silver dollar into it. "For luck," he said, folding her fingers over the coin. The unexpected warmth of her skin had him tingling all over.

She caught her breath, hesitating a moment, before dashing ahead of him to the nearest machine. She rubbed her hands together and blew on them. Then she closed her eyes. He liked the way her thick, curling lashes looked like dark moons against her pale skin as she prayed. He closed his eyes, too.

Her lashed eyes snapped open, and she looked up at him. Her face radiant, she pulled the handle.

Clink. Clink. Clink.

The machine began to blaze red and green and white.

Bingo.

He couldn't believe it. Horns honked. Sirens went off. He heard coins pouring down a chute.

She turned toward him again as a crowd formed. Not that he saw anybody but her. Not that he felt anything other than the wild, thrilling excitement in her eyes that made his blood heat.

"What happened?" she said, her voice soft with awe.

"Just like I thought. You're my lucky lady. We won."

She jumped up and down. He put his arms around her and drew her close. Again, he felt a jolt.

He didn't plan to kiss her.

It just happened, the way the best things in life do.

Her mouth was quivery and buttery soft beneath his, and instantly her sweet, melting fire surged through him. What he'd meant as a casual gesture of affection and triumph flamed into something primal and heady, something he wanted more of. He hadn't realized how lonely he'd been until now. Until her.

Her mouth opened, and he felt the tip of her tongue play with his. His entire body hardened. His heart thundered; his blood pounded in his temples. If he wasn't careful, he would embarrass himself.

Vaguely, he was aware of the crowd shouting and jostling them, of being shoved against the machine. Everything paled around the feel of her slim body mashed tightly into his, of his fierce, overwhelming arousal and desperate need to possess her. His grip tightened around her waist, and despite the circumstances, he settled her closer against his hips.

She felt good, way too good, even though she was fighting him now, twisting, pushing.

He loosened his grip, whispering, "Easy, easy. I won't hurt you."

With a sigh, the fight went out of her, and the splayed hands that had shoved at his chest muscles climbed his broad torso to his neck, her fingers twining through his hair.

"I assume you're the winning couple," somebody behind them said. "You look like honeymooners anxious to get to your hotel, so if you two will just follow me, I'll get you your money."

Honeymooners. Vegas. Quickie marriages. Hotel. Bed. He didn't like the images that flashed through his mind at the man's assumption.

Everybody laughed. Except them. Still, Connor could have gone on kissing her forever. He had never thought he would marry again. He'd thought Linda had been it, that he'd just work too hard for the rest of his life and spend as much time with Abby and Leo and little Caesar as they'd let him.

Marriage. To Anna. Crazy thought. This was a job.

His heart was still pounding lawlessly as he managed to let Anna go. "It was just a celebratory kiss," he said, putting his own finger against her soft lips. "I guess we got carried away."

"Welcome to Vegas!" a young guy in a black T-shirt shouted. "Capital of luck!"

Anna blushed. "I'd better go," she said.

"Hey… No…" When she tried to run, Connor chased her and grabbed her wrist, pulling her to him.

"We have to follow the casino manager to collect the money," he said, even as touching her again made his skin heat and his heart beat faster. "We won. *You* won."

After he collected their winnings, she refused to accept her share.

"No, it was your money. Keep it," she said.

"The least I owe you is a celebration dinner. We can argue how to split the winnings at dinner."

"No. I—I've got to go. Really. I do."

"Okay. Okay." His mind searched for something brilliant to say that would make her change her mind.

He let her go, but held her with his gaze, his grin feeling easier now. "Let's just spend tonight…together. Hey, this is Vegas. Who wants to get involved? Why don't we just have dinner…maybe see a show? What's wrong with one night? You know the old saying, strangers in the night…"

Her luminous gaze as she stared at his lips made every cell in his being quicken in warm awareness of her.

She licked her lips. "Maybe just this once…breaking my rule about not getting involved wouldn't hurt."

Two

Connor had asked for an intimate table when he'd made dinner reservations for two at the Bellagio's most popular and most expensive restaurant, and he was not disappointed by the cozy nook where he and Anna sat across a small table from each other. A great burst of flowers adorned each table. Original Picasso oil paintings hung on the walls. Six waiters hovered at a discreet distance.

"This is nice," Anna said, clearly impressed.

Connor saw no reason to tell her the chef had won countless awards. "I hope you're hungry," was all he said.

She smiled. "Starved. But the menu is so complicated, I'm not sure what to order."

"What if I order for both of us?"

She nodded.

She was easier to talk to over the dimly lit dinner. He,

however, kept losing the thread of their conversation because he ached so badly to touch her again.

Finally, unable to resist, he reached across the table and caressed her hair. To his surprise, she held on to his hand and pressed it to her cheek. When she kissed his fingers, each one, slowly, wetly, his heart thundered with all the painful needs he hadn't let himself feel these past two years.

The light went out of her eyes. "Don't ever lie to me," she said in a more serious vein. "The guy I told you about, my boyfriend, was a liar. That was the first thing that should have warned me about him."

"Right." Conner's grin no longer felt so easy.

Again he wished he'd begun dating. Too late now. God, he wanted to kiss her again. But not in a restaurant. Somewhere where they could be alone, in case things escalated.

In case. Who was he kidding?

At his hotel suite at the Bellagio, when he started kissing her outside his bedroom door, she tensed for the first time that evening.

He said, "*You* kiss *me* then. We won't do anything you don't want to do."

"That's what I'm afraid of." She lifted her mouth to his and kissed him until he was too aroused to stand more, and that hadn't been more than a kiss or two. He wrapped his arms around her and told her to stop.

"I want to sleep fully dressed in your arms with all the lights on," she said.

"You're testing me, right?"

"No. I want to be with you…but…I'm not ready for more."

On a groan he nodded. "Okay."

He lay awake for hours, holding her, wanting her. It was

nearly dawn when she leaned over and kissed him, her lips tentative against his cheek, and yet so warm when they finally grazed his mouth, he felt like he was in a furnace.

"What are you doing?" he asked.

"I'm wondering if a person can change. If it's true what you said…that anything's possible. Maybe I could be a real, certified teacher someday. Maybe I could meet a decent man. Maybe I should trust this…trust you."

"Sweetheart, you can be anything you want to be and have anything you want." At least that wasn't a lie. After all, she was an heiress. The missing Golden Spurs heiress. She had the kind of family waiting for her back in Texas that could open all the right doors.

"Show me," she whispered, kissing him again. "I want to learn how to trust."

Her mouth settled on his as if it belonged there. A long time later her tongue blazed a trail from his lips, down his throat, to his navel. She glanced up at him, her brilliant eyes wanting more.

He didn't know what the hell he wanted anymore—other than to make love to her.

He'd worry about the trip to Texas and telling Anna the truth…and all the fallout from that later.

He had to have her now.

Two weeks later

"You are so beautiful," he breathed, his drawl husky with longing.

The intense heat of Anna's desire was ebbing a little as

Connor climbed toward his. She felt blissfully, happily complete with his large, muscular body pushing into her.

One hand around his neck, she lifted her other and furtively admired the white sparkle of diamonds that proved she was his wife.

Married.

They'd done the quickie wedding chapel route, but with flare. They'd had the stretch limo, champagne, strawberries. She'd worn a strapless white wedding gown and the fox coat he'd bought her with their jackpot winnings. He'd worn a tux and a white tie. Their clothes, even the fur coat, lay in a heap beside his bed.

He buried his mouth in her hair as he plunged into her harder. Breathless, she kissed his cheek, his neck, and held on tight.

After two wonderful weeks of dinners and shows and long rides and walks in the desert, Anna couldn't believe they were really married. And yet she could. Nothing in her whole life had ever felt right until him. For the first time ever she felt a soul-deep closeness to another person, and she was willing to risk everything.

Breathing hard, clutching her closer, Connor cried out as he spilled himself into her. She clung to him, kissed his feverishly hot throat, savored his smell and the salty taste of his damp skin.

He was strong, but she didn't feel crushed or smothered. She felt almost…almost safe…for the first time…ever.

"Becky," he whispered, clutching her tightly, his body shuddering. He kissed her brow, her lips. Then he rolled off her and pulled her close.

Becky. The name touched a nerve as it had in the airport. As she lay in the dark against his long body, she trembled.

She didn't say anything, though, and soon he fell asleep with his arms around her, his warm body still pressing into hers.

Becky? Why had he called her that—again? Did she really remind him of someone? Why did the name make her feel so...so what? Strange? It seemed so familiar somehow. Why?

It didn't matter, she told herself. She loved him. He loved her. And tomorrow he was taking her home to Texas to meet his family.

Becky. As she lay in the dark beside him, the name echoed in her heart and mind, awakening a niggling doubt. Shaking a little, she twisted around so that she lay facing Connor. Staring at his harshly chiseled cheekbones and jaw, relaxed now as he slept, she took a deep, reassuring breath.

He made her feel so safe. Every time she'd awakened from a bad dream, he'd taken her in his arms and consoled her. If anyone threatened her, surely he would protect her.

Connor had said he was a rancher, but she'd noticed his steely gaze on her before he'd chased her down with her boarding pass. She'd been on guard, of course, because of that P.I. who'd shown up in Santa Fe. After she'd relaxed, she'd liked that Connor was a cowboy, that he wore that big Stetson, those butt-hugging jeans, the sheepskin jacket and the tall, black sharkskin boots.

Even now, with his thickly lashed eyes closed and his expression peaceful, he looked a little dangerous. Maybe his touch was deliberately gentle, but his big body was lean and hard, his strong hands callused. He was a rugged man. Not a man to cross. She shivered as she realized how briefly she'd known him.

A lock of heavy blond hair fell across his brow. She was about to smooth it back when she realized she didn't want to risk awakening him. He'd seemed a little tense when he'd told her he'd planned a big day for her tomorrow. His eyes had refused to meet hers when he'd told her his brother, Leo, and his wife, Abby, would meet their plane in Houston. He'd hesitated before saying, "Everybody's going to be so thrilled to meet you."

"Won't their loyalties be to Linda?"

"There's a place in their hearts for her, but they will love you, too. They already do."

"But they don't even know me."

Again, some hesitation and the worrisome note in his low tone. "Trust me, I…I have so much to tell you…about them. But they'll love you, and you'll love them. Everything will be great. I'm sure of it."

She hoped so. She didn't have a family or even a memory of one, didn't know how to be part of a family. Even before Dwight, trust had never come easily to her.

She'd gone to a psychologist a few years back because of her nightmares. He had hinted that the reason she had trouble forming close attachments might have been because she didn't know who or where her real family was. Because she didn't remember how she'd wound up on the grounds of St. Christopher's Prayer Retreat in southern Louisiana one stormy night as a small child, lost and alone.

The first eight or nine years of her life were simply gone. Her earliest memory was of Sister Kate standing just inside those tall, white walls. Her wrinkled face had been wreathed in smiles as she'd held out her arms to that frightened little girl who'd been lost in the dark.

The nuns had asked her who she was, but she hadn't known. They'd thought her memory would come back with time. It hadn't.

Other than the occasional recurring nightmares—which her psychologist had thought might have had to do with her forgotten past—she couldn't remember anything before Sister Kate.

The nuns had tried to find her family and failed. Nobody had ever cared enough to come looking for her. So she'd grown up at the prayer retreat. Sister Kate, who was dead now, had been her only family.

Becky. Strange how that name felt familiar and yet…baffling.

Feeling too unsettled all of a sudden to lie still, but not wanting to awaken Connor, Anna rose and padded across the moonlit bedroom to the bathroom. After splashing warm water on her face and drinking a tall glass of cool water, she felt more alert than ever. It was going to be one of those long nights.

Slipping her arms into the thick sleeves of her black-and-gold velour robe, she walked into the living room. She would miss this gorgeous place. They'd spent the better part of the past two weeks naked together in the snug, sumptuous master bedroom in this vast suite at the Hotel Bellagio.

Her gaze drifted to the L-shaped bar and then to the fireplace. Going to the fridge at the bar, she opened it and took out an apple. Biting into it and finding it crisp, cold and tart, she smiled. Connor had called her his pretty monkey because she loved fruit so much.

For the first two days and nights his Stetson and sheepskin jacket had lain on the bedside table. Okay, so he wasn't the neatest guy in the universe. She didn't care.

He'd ordered their meals sent up along with baskets of fruit. He hadn't stacked the dishes, either. He'd been too busy making love to her, and always they'd shared more than their bodies. Afterward, they'd talked and laughed, expressing their thoughts, their dreams. Not that she'd opened up to him completely. But did that matter? She had a lifetime to learn how to share with another person.

They'd made love, eaten chocolate and drunk champagne, and on rare occasions, they'd lain side by side contentedly reading their books. Although how anyone could like thrillers she couldn't imagine.

Anna sank onto the couch. She set her apple down, then picked up a magazine and thumbed idly through it. When the articles failed to catch her interest, she lifted the book Connor had been reading off the coffee table and opened it to the first page. An FBI agent was tracking a serial killer who kidnapped little girls and did terrible things to them. With a horrified gasp, she slammed the book shut and flung it back onto the table, but as she did so, a business card and a tattered black-and-white snapshot of two little girls in pigtails on a horse fluttered to the floor.

Absently she picked up the card and photograph. A smile lifted her lips as she saw her husband's name, Connor Storm. Then, as she read further, her smile froze. *Storm Investigations*. Slowly, oh so slowly, every part of her congealed until she felt like an ice statue, sitting there and staring mutely at the name of his security firm.

He wasn't a rancher. She remembered how Connor had watched her so intently in the airport while pretending not to; how she'd suspected him of taking her boarding pass as a ruse to meet her.

How could she have been so stupid—again? She began to shake—with rage or fear, she didn't know. Her heart pounded. She sucked in a breath and then another.

How could she have let herself trust a tough guy like Connor when she'd known someone was after her?

Because the P.I. who'd showed up at the school had given a Spanish surname. He'd been tall and dark with a tiny scar on his cheek. Still…

She was so upset, she barely glanced at the photograph. Carrying Connor's business card, she got up and walked across the room to the gilt desk where Connor's laptop was set up. Beside his computer was a large white envelope that contained a dozen eight-by-tens of their wedding, pictures she'd thought she would treasure.

While she waited for the computer to boot, she ripped the envelope open. The first picture was of her snuggled against Connor in front of the stretch limo. His golden head was bent over hers.

She touched her lips, remembering his kiss. She'd been so happy then; felt so safe and protected. And it had all been a lie.

Rage at his betrayal made her clench her fists. Then grief at the thought of the bleakness of a future without him froze her. She took a deep breath. She would get over this.

A tear spilled over her lashes. Wiping it away, she deliberately tore each picture in two and let the pieces fall to the floor. Her throat tight, her eyes hot and wet, the pain in her chest acute, she turned back to the computer. She closed her eyes and then opened them.

Her fingers shook as she began typing in the Web address that was at the bottom of Connor's business card.

Instantly an impressive page lit up the monitor. She didn't have to read much before she knew Connor Storm was the last thing from a harmless, tenderhearted, grieving, widowed rancher.

No! Her lying snake of a husband owned a huge security company that was based in Houston, but had branches in other cities. He specialized in finding missing persons.

Not that he wasn't into all aspects of the security business. The guy was a major talent in his field. He was obviously an extremely wealthy and successful man. One with a reputation for being tough as nails, for being relentless when it came to finding missing persons.

She read one father's testimonial. "The police couldn't help us when Ethan vanished. Connor Storm led the search and found him half-starved, tied up in a warehouse cellar. The police were following a false lead. I owe my son's life to the man."

For some reason she couldn't stop thinking about that poor, frightened little boy. Or about Connor himself, who was quoted in the testimonial as saying, "My mission is to help families who would never get closure without the service of a private investigator. I can't always give everybody a happy ending, but I can usually give them the truth. From there a person can begin to rebuild."

He wasn't all bad if he'd saved that little boy.

Her mind flashed back to the night she'd been alone in woods outside St. Christopher's.

Okay, so maybe Connor wasn't a total villain, but he was a liar. He'd had no right to court her under false pretenses. Why had he gone so far? What did he want?

"I don't care why Connor did any of it! I can't care why!" She clenched her hands into fists again. When would she ever learn?

Slowly, carefully she removed the diamond rings that Connor had placed so lovingly on her finger a few hours earlier and set them on the desk.

Tears streamed down her cheeks as she opened up his word processing program and began typing.

I loved you. I trusted you. And you tricked me. How could you go so far as to marry me? I don't know what the truth is between us. But whatever was between us is over now.

If you loved me even a little, let me be me. Don't ever try to find me. Just let me go.
Anna

She hit the print button. Savagely, she dried her eyes with the back of her hands as she waited on the printer. She had to be strong. She had to forget him. Slowly, her weary brain began to form a plan.

Payback time.

She laid her printed farewell note on the desk. Then she yanked the plug out of his computer and threw the computer into a red-and-white duffel bag. She grabbed his tux jacket and his wallet and stuffed them in her bag, too.

Then she grabbed the rest of his clothes. Wadding them up, she jammed them inside the bag.

She'd leave him nothing to wear. Without money or clothes, it would take him a while to regroup and chase her.

Three

Houston, Texas

One minute Connor was drumming his pencil on his desk as he tried to concentrate on one of Guerra's routine surveillance reports, and the next, a telephone ring buzzed from his computer.

Leo.

Nobody else ever used Skype to reach him.

Connor grabbed his mouse. Sure enough, Leo's name was blinking at the bottom of his monitor.

Connor accepted the call and turned on his Webcam. A few seconds later Leo's tanned face filled his screen. His mouth was thin, his jaw set, his black eyes hard. Something was up.

Connor smiled, even though he was suddenly edgy as hell. "How can I help you, big brother?"

Leo came to the point. "The agency I hired to find Becky after I fired *you* has located her."

After I fired you. Connor ground his teeth. He hated being reminded that he'd failed his brother eighteen months ago.

"You found Anna?" Surprise, and the abrupt acceleration of a savage pulse in his temple, made his voice harsh. "Good for you."

The memory of the way Anna had left him without even giving him a chance to defend himself was never far from his mind. Like a lust-sodden fool, he'd jumped out of bed when he realized she wasn't nestled behind him. Finding the suite empty, he'd feared the worst—that she'd been hurt or taken. He'd been in hell until he'd stumbled onto those shredded wedding pictures and the cryptic note that had cut his heart out.

I trusted you...you tricked me.... Whatever was between us is over now.

Over. Hell, yes, it was over!

She'd taken his computer, briefcase, wallet and clothes. He'd had sensitive data on that laptop, which she'd jeopardized, causing important clients to bail.

He'd failed Leo. Leo had been so furious he'd balked at first about wiring him the money he'd needed to get out of Vegas.

He'd failed Abby, too. When he'd handed her the torn wedding pictures, she'd wept and stared at those of her sister for hours. "She's alive."

Those pictures and the DNA he'd taken from the suite proved that.

Leo had fired him and demanded the hefty retainer the

Golden Spurs bunch had paid him. The two brothers hadn't spoken for months. Terence, Abby's father, had flown in from South America and cussed him out, too.

Abby had finally intervened and forced Leo and Terence to forgive him. Not that Connor could forgive himself. He'd let a lot of people down, important people, people he cared about.

Shutting off his memories, Connor focused on his brother's face on the computer screen.

"I thought you'd want to know where your wife is," Leo said.

"Well, I don't, and I'm surprised you'd confide the news to me, since I screwed up so royally."

"You damn sure did, but that's over and done with. I've forgiven you, so forgive yourself. Becky paid you back— leaving you in that hotel suite with nothing to wear but your birthday suit, not to mention dumping your computer and wallet and clothes in that Dumpster behind the hotel."

A waiter had seen her march out to the Dumpster and heave his stuff into the garbage. The guy had snatched Connor's computer, which had contained all that highly sensitive information. The bum had also stolen Connor's ID and had bought a Lexus. The rat was living it up in a five-star hotel in New York when one of Connor's men had caught up with him.

Yes, she'd paid him back. His men were still cracking jokes behind his back about it.

"She's in New Orleans," Leo said.

"I don't care!" When the painful pulse in his temple sped up, his fingers tightened on the mouse. He needed to end this session ASAP.

"A tree fell on the place she's been working. She's been a caregiver to an old lady named Gabrielle Cyr. The old lady died, so Becky will be moving on if we don't grab her fast. Story about the tree and the old lady, who's sort of famous, made the national news, which was how my guy found her. So—if you want your wife back, I thought I'd let you pick her up and bring her home for us. Only this time, don't screw it up."

"Me? Pick her up? Not my job. You fired me, remember? I feel bad that I messed things up for you the last time. Bad that I ever got involved with her. If I saw her, I might strangle her."

"I don't think so." Leo's black eyes narrowed. He stroked his chin thoughtfully. "There's more."

"Spit it out."

Leo's voice was so dark suddenly Connor's blood was beating violently. He remembered Linda's ashen face in the hospital and his feelings of helplessness as he'd touched her cool, lifeless cheek and then stared at all the tubes attached to her.

An icy hand seemed to grab him by the throat and squeeze hard.

"Anna? Is she hurt? She'd better be all right! Tell me, damn it!"

"She had a baby. A little girl. The kid is nine months old. She's got your dimple and your blond hair. You do the math."

Then Leo held up a picture of the cutest kid in the universe.

Her baby? Gone?

Anna, who went by Sue now, stared at Taylor's empty

crib. She set the last stack of newspapers that she'd been about to carry out to the back porch down beside it.

Her baby was gone!

Where could Taylor be? It wasn't like a nine-month-old could get up and go off by herself. With two women working in the house, herself and Josette, Anna had thought Taylor was safe. Their neighborhood was so quiet and peaceful, she hadn't locked the doors.

Anna took a deep breath. She glanced down at her watch and tried to remember when she'd last checked on Taylor after she'd put her down for her nap. Surely she hadn't been carrying newspapers out to the back porch more than a few minutes.

She hadn't heard a car or the doorbell. When footsteps resounded above her, she remembered Josette again, who was supposed to be upstairs cleaning. Maybe Josette had her. Doubtful, but maybe.

Anna rushed out of the room and ran up the staircase, which looked much better now that it was clear of newspapers and magazines. Not that she cared now.

Gabrielle Cyr had been a pack rat, and she'd had ninety years to hone her skill. After her burial yesterday, the family had left orders for Josette and her to clean out the ancient plantation house so it could be put on the market.

. Josette's plump form knelt in the bathroom, placing bottles of shampoo and packages of soap in cardboard boxes. There had to be twenty-five bottles of shampoo in this bathroom alone. Huge trash bags brimmed with garbage.

"Have you seen Taylor anywhere?" Anna cried.

Josette turned, her round, kindly face blank as she arched her back and rubbed it in the joint that had arthritis.

"Taylor?" Picking up on Anna's emotion, Josette frowned. "*La petite* is napping in her little bed, *non, chère?*"

"Oh, God. *Non. Non.*"

Josette's big brown eyes clouded. "Don't you worry, *non.* I'll help you look for her, yes? We find her."

"Yes, you check the upstairs. I'll check downstairs and the grounds," Anna said.

"And go next door. Maybe Mr. Denis, he take her?"

The old man liked to rock the baby on the porch. Denis was slightly senile, not to mention upset by the funeral of his oldest friend, but surely not even he would take Taylor without asking. He'd certainly never done so before.

It was ironic. Anna had taken the job of caring for Gabrielle, an old lady of esteemed Creole lineage, because she never had to leave her baby to work.

And now—this!

By the time Anna had checked the house and the grounds without finding Taylor, her heart had really begun to race. Rushing back into her baby's room, the sight of Taylor's empty crib made her feel sick and so light-headed, she was afraid she'd faint. But she couldn't faint. She had to find Taylor.

Where could Taylor be? Dwight? Anna couldn't imagine Dwight having any interest in her baby. He'd wanted her, but her alone. And that had been a while ago. So that left Connor, who had real rights to Taylor.

Connor was a P.I. She'd read his Web page often enough to know that he was good at what he did. The thought of that lying snake showing up here and finding her baby made her heart pound.

Anna went to the telephone to call 911, but even before she lifted it from its cradle, she remembered the family had had it disconnected. There was nothing for it but to go get her own phone in the car where she'd left it after the trip from the cemetery.

Grabbing her car keys, Anna raced through the house and back down the stairs. It was the first of June and unseasonably cool. A whisper of humid air stole as slowly as dripping molasses across the porch. The faint breeze feathered the leaves in the tops of the trees, making the moss float like chiffon banners above the emerald-green lawn.

Fluttering yellow tape roped off the collapsed wall and scattered debris as she ran toward the garage. Rusty scaffolding surrounded one of Belle Terre's shattered columns.

Anna had thought this had been the perfect job until a week ago when the hurricane-damaged tree had fallen on the house, sending bricks and debris through Belle Terre's large windows. Then Gabrielle had died. And now Taylor was missing.

Suddenly Anna wished she'd taken any job but this one.

Did the television coverage have something to do with Taylor being gone? All that excitement when the crews had arrived to interview the old lady had proved too much for Gabrielle, and three days later she'd died.

The garage was dark, but when Anna threw open the door of her Honda the interior light came on. Sure enough, her phone lay on the passenger seat, but when she picked it up and started punching buttons, she saw the battery was dead.

Seizing her phone charger off the floor, she plugged one end into her phone and the other into her cigarette lighter. Then she turned the key in the ignition and stomped on the gas. Instead of starting, the Honda made a weird spinning noise.

She clamped her eyes shut, crossed herself and prayed before jiggling the key and ramming her big toe on the gas pedal again. Same whirring noise! She slammed her hands against the steering wheel.

"One more time! Third time's gonna be the charm." She was reaching for the key when a glance into her rearview mirror revealed a tall, broad-shouldered man wearing a Stetson. His long, jean-clad legs thrust widely apart, he stood backlighted in a beam of fiery sunlight that shot through her open garage doors. Red fire lit a lock of his golden hair that curled waywardly against his starched white collar.

Connor.

He wore a white long-sleeved shirt and the same black sharkskin boots. In his right hand he held an ominous-looking metal object.

Where's Taylor?

Her heart beating wildly, she sprang out of the driver's seat. His chiseled face was set, his eyes as frigidly blue as polar ice chips. If ever a man looked poised for a fight, he did.

In that first horrible moment of mutual recognition, a wellspring of confusing emotion swept Anna. She'd loved him. And he'd lied and lied and lied. Worst of all, he was probably here because he thought he could take Taylor away from her.

"Where's Taylor?"

"This is your spark plug coil wire, sweetheart," he said, his deep tone impersonal. "Until I put it back, I'm afraid you're stuck here. With me. We've got a few things to talk about."

"Where's—"

"—our baby?"

His deadly grin made her shiver.

He knew.

He looked so hard and yet so infuriatingly cocky, anger swamped her fear.

Suddenly she felt like rushing him. She wanted to kick his shin or at least stomp on his toe…to break something.

"She's with your friend…in the house."

"Josette?"

He nodded.

"You took her?"

"Let's just say we took a walk to admire some leaves and worms and a black-and-white puppy that licked our faces. It's about time we spent a little quality time getting to know each other, don't you think?"

"You had no right to come here," she whispered, backing away from him toward the side door of the garage.

"No right to visit my own child? I'm still your husband, remember? Taylor's father?"

His words coupled with his hot gaze stirred unwanted memories and caused disturbing erotic sensations that made her blood heat even though she was determined to hate him.

"I wrote you in that note that it was over," she snapped.

"Maybe for you, sweetheart," he said, his long legs moving swiftly through the eerie shadows of her garage. "What about Taylor? And what if I disagree? I'm half the equation."

"This isn't math. I don't want to be married to you."

"Well, you are."

"You couldn't possibly want to be married to me, either."

"Couldn't I?" His devouring gaze shot from her face down her body. "You're a beautiful woman. Maybe I can't forget those fourteen happy days. And happier nights."

Nights. That last word scalded her. "You lied to me. Everything you did, everything you said was a lie."

"Not everything, sweetheart. Besides, I had to get you back to Houston."

"Why? What's in Houston?"

"I'll tell you when we get there."

"As if I'd ever go anywhere with you now."

"You will. And so will Taylor. We're a family."

Oh, God, this was even worse than her nightmares. Suddenly all she wanted was to hold her baby in her arms. Arguing with him was accomplishing nothing. Despite the coolness of the day, the garage felt stifling.

"I want to see Taylor. I want to make sure my baby's all right."

"As if I'd hurt my own child. She's fine," he muttered angrily.

"She'd better be."

"Or you'll what? Steal my clothes and money again?"

"Whatever I did, you deserved it! You worked for Dwight!"

"The hell I did!"

Marching past him, she began sprinting toward the house as soon as he was a few feet behind her.

"Hey," he yelled.

She should have known he'd come after her. When she stumbled over a root, she would have fallen into the pile of bricks in the thick grass that lay between her and Belle Terre if he hadn't grabbed her left arm. Spinning her around, she found herself mashed into the solid wall of his muscular chest.

"Lucky for me that old tree fell, and your boss was so well-known," he said. "I quit looking for you after Vegas, but the agent my brother hired found you, thanks to the television coverage."

"Unlucky for me, though." She shoved at his chest, but it was like trying to push a granite wall. "I never wanted to see you again."

"The people who hired me to find you aren't the bad guys, you know."

"What? You worked for Dwight, right?"

She quit struggling in his arms. He'd bristled when she'd accused him of working for Dwight before.

"No."

"But you did! You had to!"

He shook his head. "No, I didn't. I'm telling the truth."

"Is that a first?"

His face hardened, but he didn't defend himself. Still, somehow, she didn't know why, but she believed him about Dwight. Not that that let him off the hook. "Well, you lied about everything else."

"And you never tell lies, *Sue! Sue* is your new alias, isn't it?"

"You're the detective. You tell me."

"I just did."

"So, if you're not working for Dwight, who were you working for? Not that I'm going to believe anything you might tell me about that, either."

"Right. So, why should I even bother?"

She pushed at his chest again. "Tell me!"

"No. It'll wait. You're not calling the shots anymore. I am."

Scary thought. Even scarier were the tingly sensations she was beginning to feel in his grasp. As long as she'd been arguing with him, she'd managed to distract herself. Yet…

While she was locked in his arms, in the deep shade of the magnolia tree, the air felt cool against her skin, a sharp contrast to the heat from his muscular body. She felt his heart beating and instantly she remembered being held in his arms that first time in the airport. More disturbing were memories of the long, sweet nights beside the fireplace, when he'd pressed her beneath him.

Every kiss, every caress, had been part of the spider-web of lies he'd woven. And yet… He'd been so sweet…his lips and hands so tender. She'd remembered him at the height of his passion, when he'd driven inside her and had seemed to lose himself completely. Could a man lie about all that? Could he?

His hand brushed a leaf out of her hair, and she shivered.

Frantic, she stared past him at the windmill palms and thick clumps of philodendron. "Don't," she began in a strangled tone.

"Careful." His deep voice was huskier now, maybe because holding her close affected him, too.

No. She didn't believe that. He'd weave a new deceptive web if she let him.

"These bricks are unstable," he said. "They could fall, and you could hurt yourself."

When the bricks she was standing on shifted, she clung to him even though she knew he was her greatest danger.

"For what it's worth, I never wanted to hurt you," he said, and then scowled as if he hadn't wanted to admit that.

Again she felt his pounding heart, his heat, and a thrilling rush of unwanted need spiraled through her. He was lying, and she was falling for it all over again.

"Let me go!" she said furiously.

"Not yet." Holding on to her hand, he led her up the stairs to the teak bench on the shattered front veranda of Belle Terre.

"I haven't been a particularly happy man since you ran out on me."

Truth or lie? She hated not knowing, as she studied the dark circles beneath his eyes and the weariness around his mouth.

He tore his gaze from hers. "Did you ever think of me— even once after you ran out?"

"I tried not to."

"So you didn't wonder what I might have been going through?"

Yes. Every single day. Every single night. The nights were the worst. All the time. I kept wondering how you could have worked for Dwight and made love to me so convincingly. I kept wondering what your game was.

"Every time I wondered, I told myself you lied to me about everything, that Dwight had hired you."

"Okay." He took a deep breath. "Like I said, I never worked for him."

"But you were working for someone."

"I returned their money. But as soon as I found out about our baby, I knew I had no choice but to come here. I want to know my child."

She squeezed her eyes shut, pressed her fingers to the bridge of her nose. "No."

"You can't stop me."

"I can't be with you. You lied. And I'm through with liars. You have to understand that. We'll get a divorce. Go our separate ways."

"It's not that simple. Other people are involved."

"The people who hired you?"

He nodded. "And then there's our own little problem. Now I know about Taylor. So all bets are off."

"You can't make me come back to you."

"Oh, yes, I can, sweetheart."

Maybe he would have elaborated, but when Taylor began to cry from inside the house, his hard face darkened with concern for their child. "Is she okay?"

Anna didn't answer. She was racing ahead of him inside the house to find out.

Four

Taylor was screaming fitfully now.

Great bursts of sound were followed by pitiful little mews. Strangely, those helpless, little shuddering sobs tore at Connor's heart as nothing else ever had before.

What was wrong with her? He'd seen people die, but this almost made him feel worse.

"Where's that damn woman I entrusted our baby to?" he thundered.

"Josette? Nearby, I'm sure." Lovingly, Anna leaned over the crib and pulled a blanket off Taylor's face.

Josette, her plump face pale, bustled into the room carrying a broom. "I just left her. *La petite,* she is okay, yes?"

"She's crying. She's not okay," Connor growled, feeling outraged by the question when his daughter was screaming her head off.

"She'd pulled a blanket over her eyes and couldn't remove it," Anna explained. "Didn't you, little darling?" she whispered tenderly down to his child.

"Is that all?" he said, feeling sheepish when the older woman smiled. Quickly, just to make sure, he joined Anna at the pink crib that was filled with rattles and colorful squeeze toys.

Taylor's face was red. Thank God, she was calmer and had stopped making those bloodcurdling noises. She was still sniffling, however, and a single tear sparkled on her cheek.

For the first time he saw his picture taped to the wall alongside Anna's behind the crib. Was that why Taylor had perked up the instant he'd walked into the nursery earlier? Had Anna made his face familiar to her?

"Darling, it's okay," Anna was saying softly. "You're safe and sound and the center of attention again."

Josette must have changed Taylor before putting her down because the baby was wearing a pink romper with yellow giraffes now. The baby turned from Anna to him, her blue eyes widening in surprise as she regarded him. Then she began to coo and gurgle flirtatiously.

"Hi, there, again," he said gently, leaning closer.

His voice brought a wide smile followed by more gurgles. *Thrill of the month.* Taylor began to kick as if she were delighted, too.

When she rolled over and began to pull up and attempt to move near him, she smiled. He smiled right back at her. Then she sat up and clapped her hands, and he clapped his, too.

"Monkey see, monkey do," he teased.

The imp beamed up at him and clapped some more.

How could that wide grin that showed off a single tooth rip out his heart? And the dimple… He'd been teased unmercifully about his dimple. On her, it was cute.

When he cupped the baby's head, which was hot and damp from crying, Anna gasped and then backed out of his way. He lifted the little girl easily and snuggled her against his shoulder and began to move about the room with her.

He'd had a lot of experience with babies in Afghanistan. Only those babies had mainly been hungry and poor and their mothers terrified out of their minds. Those babies hadn't been as plump as his or smelled of fresh detergent, baby powder and shampoo. And they hadn't tugged on his paternal heartstrings as she had from the first moment he'd seen her. He was pleased to discover Anna was such a good mother.

Watching him with their child, Anna's eyes had grown strangely luminous. Her face was radiant.

"Taylor," he cooed against the baby's cheek as he petted her head. "You're pretty…just like your mother." That last was out before he'd realized what he was saying.

He lifted his gaze to Anna's again. Her lips were trembling even as she stiffened her shoulders.

"I—I show her our pictures every day and say, 'Dada and Mama,'" she said.

"I'll bet you were sorry you couldn't get rid of me completely," he said.

She went so white, he regretted the harsh comment.

A hard lump filled his throat. Then he turned his full attention on his daughter. At least his feelings for her were simple. He was crazy about her.

How many times had he told his guys in the squadron that if you'd seen one baby, you'd seen them all?

Wrong. Taylor was the prettiest baby in the universe.

"She was born maybe nine months ago?" His voice was low. "And you didn't tell me."

"Because I thought…you were dangerous."

"So, all these months while she was learning to pull up, while she grew a tooth, I never knew. I never even thought of the possibility…" A rush of unwanted tenderness toward his daughter coupled with fierce anger toward her mother unnerved him.

"When I missed my period I—I counted the weeks after I'd left you," she said.

Fury lashed him at the bitter memory of waking up and finding her gone. Stark naked, he'd read and reread a printout of some note she'd drafted on his laptop, the laptop she'd trashed. Crushing her note in his fist, he'd stormed out into the hall without a stitch on. Without his key even. He'd caught his door right before it had slammed shut.

I loved you. I trusted you. And you tricked me…. Whatever was between us is over now. Connor had memorized her damn note on the spot.

"Were you ever going to get around to telling me about her?" he asked, keeping his tone polite and easy for Taylor's sake, even though he already knew the answer.

"No. I figured we were better off without you."

"Right." Rage flared up within him, but when Taylor reached out and touched his cheek with her soft little fingers, then smiled at him, he fought to control it.

"Da…da…coo…"

His daughter was a genius. With such a brilliant little girl, it was hard to stay totally furious at her mother. Still, he gave it his best.

"Well, you're not better off."

In her faded jeans and ancient blue sweater, Anna was every bit as shabby as her surroundings. Her loafers were scuffed, their heels worn. It was all too obvious she couldn't afford to spend a dime on herself.

"Is this really how you want to live? How you want Taylor to live?"

She stiffened with pride. "I have…had…a job. We have what we need," she said.

"Minimum wage? You get paid in cash? That's not a real job. You're part of the underground economy. You live like this so you can stay under the radar, don't you? Because it makes it easy to hide?"

She cast her eyes down. "I was worried about Dwight and you."

"I never worked for that jerk!"

Connor glanced at the room. The mansion had seen better days. The paint was chipped and yellowed. Bits of faded floral wallpaper curled at the seams. The oak floor was scarred and the cheap, red throw carpets that hid most of it were dirty and threadbare. Taylor's crib was scratched and wobbly. Its pink linens were so thin he could see the mattress through them. Stuffing exploded from the uphol-stered rocking chair in the corner.

Carrying Taylor, he began to pace. He remembered that single red-and-white duffel bag Anna had had in Vegas. It had been snowing outside, but she hadn't even owned a jacket, which was why he'd bought her the fox coat in

Vegas. Against her wishes, he'd bought her an entire new wardrobe, which she'd left behind; which he'd packed and mailed to Houston and stored even though he'd never wanted to see her again.

Since she'd been living on the run, she probably didn't want nice things or friends that would call attention to herself. He stopped in front of her dresser. When her eyes widened with alarm, he yanked the top drawer open.

"No!" she cried out.

He smiled grimly when he saw her stash of hundred-dollar bills and a Louisiana driver's license with her picture and the name Sue Oakley on it. He sifted through the bills until he found a social security card with the same name.

"Fake IDs. Paid cash for them, a lot of cash, I bet. Not so easy to get, are they?" When she didn't answer, he grabbed the driver's license and the social security card. As he was about the stick the IDs into his back pocket, she made a grab for them.

"What are you doing?" she said. "Those are mine. You can't take them."

"I already did." Still holding Taylor, he stared down at Anna. "You know something that's haunted me? All these months I kept remembering how your eyes shone when you told me you wanted to be a teacher."

She swallowed.

"Was that a lie?"

She shook her head. "It's not really a practical idea now, though, when it's hard enough for me to support—"

"Right. You can't ever be anything like that if you can't stay in one place, if you have to be paid cash like an illegal immigrant, if you always have to use fake IDs. Did it ever occur to you that unless you change, Taylor won't have much of a future, either?"

The color leached from her thin face.

Turning away from her, he cradled Taylor closer against his chest. Anna's lifestyle was sad enough for her, but the thought of Taylor being dragged from place to place…of Taylor changing names and identities again and again…of Taylor never knowing him, her father…never being able to stay in a school she liked or a town she felt at home in…

He wasn't about to allow Taylor to grow up like that. "You have a family in Texas. I was working for them," he said.

"What? I don't have a family." Her eyes shone too vividly in her pale face.

"You do. You were…er…lost when you were just a kid. Your sister and adoptive father have been looking for you ever since. More recently your biological father's family, the Kembles, joined in the search. Basically, I was working for the entire bunch."

"Don't do this. Don't tell any more lies…just to manipulate me."

"Right. I'm a liar." He took a breath. "Okay, we won't talk about them just yet. But Taylor needs to know her family."

"*Her family? I'm* her family!"

"Do you think you're enough? Do you want to be alone the rest of your life? What was I *just* saying to you?"

Anna staring at him wildly, and maybe he couldn't totally blame her, since he'd been less than straight with her in Vegas.

"I didn't have a father," Connor said, deciding to take a different perspective. "So, I learned the hard way what it was like to be a nobody in strange towns. My brother,

Leo, got a neighbor girl pregnant. Our mother's boss threw us off his ranch because the girl was supposed to be his son's girlfriend. I was fifteen. My mother died a few months later. Leo had to scramble to get through college and put food on our table."

He stopped. Anna didn't care about him. So why was he boring her with the story of his life? Why was he telling her how it was to be friendless in a new school? Why try to explain why he'd started running with a bad crowd? It couldn't possibly matter to her that he'd been hell-bound until Leo had talked him into the military. And Linda… He'd sunk to the bottom again after her death.

"What good will a mother like you be to Taylor when she's older, if all you know how to do is run from your own shadow? I bet you'll abandon her someday, the same way you ran out on me."

"No! I would never do that!"

"What if, God forbid, something happens to you?"

"It won't."

"I wish I knew that for sure," he said. "Being a single mom, raising a kid on your own—that's tough in the best of circumstances."

"I wouldn't ever leave Taylor."

"Taylor needs a world larger than you could ever give her."

The blood drained from Anna's face. Feeling more empathy for the mother of his child than he wanted to, he brushed Taylor's cheek with his hand, and she began sucking on his little finger. A shock of warm, paternal emotion went through him.

"Is she hungry?" he asked.

"I want my driver's license and social security card back."

He shook his head and repeated the question. "Is she hungry?"

"Probably. But she's so fascinated by you, she's temporarily distracted."

"Does she breast-feed?"

Her quick blush told him the answer was yes even before she nodded.

Not having realized the intimacy of his question until he'd asked it, his eyes met Anna's, and that part of him that was fighting to build boundaries against her faltered again.

His heart ached. Damn her for this visceral connection.

His own face and neck felt so hot, he had to yank at his collar. Except for her full breasts, she was thinner than she'd been in Vegas and much more vulnerable-looking.

Was she worn ragged from caring for the old lady, this big house and their baby, too? Obviously she needed his help more than she would admit.

He imagined her in the rocking chair with Taylor after the old woman had gone to bed. If she came home with him, he'd take care of them, provide nannies and sitters and later, lessons and private schools. He'd give his kid everything he'd done without.

She shut her eyes against his gaze briefly, probably because she couldn't bear looking at him.

"Anna, I won't let you vanish and leave me all alone, wondering where the two of you are, wondering if you're safe. What if I did something like that to you? What if I kept her? How would that feel?"

On a sob, she grabbed Taylor from him. "Don't—" A single tear splashed down her cheek. "Don't even think it!"

He hated making her cry, yet she didn't deny that what he said was her intent. Anger filled him.

No way could he let Taylor go. Or her, either. Not until a lot of important issues had been settled. Like taking her back to her family. Like establishing his custodial rights.

Her fierce desire to run and hide from him made him feel helpless and out of control. He knew from Afghanistan that whenever he'd had that I-have-nothing-to-lose attitude, he was at his most dangerous to himself and others.

"Don't push me," he whispered. "Forget about a divorce. Just come home with me so we can work this mess out."

When she flinched and then clung to Taylor, the baby squawking at the closeness, his stomach tightened.

"No," she gasped. "I can't. Please—"

"*Yes*. You can. You must." He strode to her and towered over her. "You think I can't see that you're living on the edge, barely making it. This place is a dump. You don't have an education. I do. Besides that, I'm wealthy and well-connected. I can give Taylor a normal life. As my wife, you could have time to make something of yourself…to go to college…become a teacher."

"I don't want to be married to you or to live with you."

He pulled out her fake social security card. "Would you prefer jail?"

"I haven't done anything wrong."

"You've been working with fake IDs, which means you've broken the law. What if I turn you in?"

"You wouldn't dare!" Anna sank into the rocker, her knees giving way.

"Don't push your luck. What if I give the authorities Ms. Oakley's fake driver's license and social security card? Have you ever heard of identity theft? Did you ever wonder if these items are legitimate and belong to other people? Or if you've paid criminals to make them? Identity theft is a personal issue with me. Because of you, a crook found my wallet in that Dumpster where you threw it and stole *my* identity. I'm just now getting it all sorted out."

"Please…."

"What if I tell the authorities your employers have been paying you in cash? You'll get in even more trouble if you haven't reported all your income, won't you? So will your employers. They'll have to hire attorneys, who'll charge them far more than you ever earned."

"But they were only trying to help me out."

"There are laws about paying taxes and filling out the correct forms, you know. Did you obey all those laws? Did they? You can commit murder and get away with it more easily than you can cheat the IRS."

"I'm a good person. I was only doing what I had to—to survive."

"Right. You *had* to steal my child. You *had* to work under an assumed name that might have been stolen from somebody else. Trust me, the judges have heard it all before."

"But you know Dwight was after me! You're twisting everything! You wouldn't dare turn me in!"

"That's where you're wrong, *Ms. Oakley*." He sank to his knees and touched the back of Taylor's head. Then he looked up at Anna. His voice softened. "I would do anything to get my child. I can afford the best lawyers. And don't think I wouldn't make sure I got sole custody of

Taylor while you fought your legal battles with money you don't have and then served your time."

"Served my time?" Her voice sounded hollow as she clutched Taylor tighter.

"My lawyer might very well find a way to have you declared unfit."

"I'm not unfit."

"Maybe that's not for you to decide—once we get the law involved. I'm going to tell you something, sweetheart. Money buys a lot of what passes for justice in this country. I've got money, lots of it. You don't."

"I hate you. I'll hate you forever."

"But you're a survivor, so that won't stop you from coming home with me and living with me as my wife now that you see how it's to your advantage, now, will it?" He pushed back his Stetson. "Because if you do that, sweetheart—and *only* if you do that—I'll keep all your dirty little secrets. And I'll do everything in my power to protect you from Dwight if he pops back into your life."

She glared up at him. Her lips were thin, her eyes flat. He didn't want to know what she was thinking. He was glad she merely grimaced and remained silent. When she offered no further arguments, he began to relax a little.

"So, as soon as you feed *our* baby, I suggest you start packing. We leave for Houston—tonight—where we will live together as husband and wife."

"I don't like being forced."

"I don't like a lot of things about this situation, either. Tomorrow we'll talk about the people who hired me to find you—your family."

She flinched.

"And, sweetheart, if I bring you back as my wife, I will be civil to you in public, and I will expect the same courtesy."

She closed her eyes, refusing to look at him. "I don't believe this," she whispered. "I don't believe any of this."

"I know it's a lot to digest, but nod if you agree to my terms."

He'd almost given up on getting an answer when her chin dipped ever so slightly.

Finally, a yes. He hated this situation as much as she did. But she'd taken his child and kept her from him, and his anger was out of control.

Five

"When I asked you to be civil, I meant it," Connor said, as he led Anna down the stairs into his Houston bedroom.

"There's nobody here but you and me," she whispered. "Surely you don't expect me to act when we're alone."

"You prefer to live like we're in a war zone?"

"Nothing about this situation is about what I prefer, now, is it?" Stiffening, Anna crossed her arms over her soft, full breasts, maybe because his gaze had lingered there once too often.

"I won't sleep with you," she said, as she stared at his vast chrome bed with the pale satin sheets and numerous pillows.

They were standing in Connor's sunken bedroom in his midcentury modern mansion on the Buffalo Bayou, which was located in one of the most prestigious neighborhood in Houston's inner loop. Not that she'd acted the least bit impressed with his mansion as most people had ever since he'd had the best designer in town do an outrageously expensive redo.

Hell, after they'd tucked Taylor into her crib, her only comment as she'd followed him up and down the floating white marble steps that lacked railings was that his three-story home was the furthest thing from child-friendly.

"We'll worry about that when Taylor's a toddler," he'd replied, his words implying they had that much of a future, which he very much doubted.

"I want my own room," she blurted, turning away from his bed. "Sleeping with you down here is not an acceptable arrangement."

He moved in front of the steps, barring her escape.

"You're my wife and all that implies. So you'll stay here with me and do as I say."

"You caveman, me cavegirl?"

"Your interpretation—not mine, but then…whatever lights your fire."

"I can't believe you're so crude or that you're doing this—forcing me…."

Her accusatory attitude annoyed the hell out of him. She was the one who'd stolen his child. "Maybe you forced me. Ever consider my side?"

She bit her lip. Clearly she hadn't. She didn't give enough of a damn.

Goaded, he raked his gaze slowly down her luscious curves, not stopping at her waist, but moving lower, even when she gasped and turned an angry shade of red.

"If it's sex you're worried about, you can relax, sweetheart," he said. "I'm not in the mood…at least not tonight."

Liar. He'd burn in hell for that one. Her nearness in his bedroom after going without for so long had him turned on.

"The only reason I want you in my bed is because I don't trust you enough to let you out of my sight," he said. "And since this child-unfriendly bedroom doesn't even have a door I can lock, I want you beside me all night."

"So we're you prisoners? You're kidnapping us?"

The word *kidnapping* hit him hard. The accusation made his heart speed up and her face blur. Obviously, she remembered next to nothing about what had happened to her. He swallowed a long breath.

Floor-to-ceiling glass walls allowed intimate views of a lush backyard that was full of greenery and flowers, a curve of brown bayou and the rectangular swimming pool. He leaned against a wall and pushed a button that made tall, gauzy draperies swish closed. He didn't think anybody was watching their angry exchange, but he wanted complete privacy just the same.

"Because of my daughter, *I'm* just as much *your* prisoner." His voice was low, deliberately controlled. "You may be her mother, but I have rights, too. If you're determined to split up with me, I intend to make sure I get a fair custody hearing. So—if you want to call the law, go ahead. Better yet, I'll do it for you. Believe me, I have a thing or two to tell them about you."

She paled as he grabbed his phone.

"Sweetheart, if you think the cops are going to let you walk out of here with my baby after the stunts you've pulled, you're more naive about the legal system than I think a smooth little operator would be." His eyes were glued to her face as he jabbed the miniature keypad.

His hands were big and the keys tiny, so he hit a lot of wrong numbers. So what? He was bluffing.

"No!" Holding up a shaking hand, she ran toward him and grabbed for the phone. "Don't you dare call them! I'll do…whatever you want. Anything…even…well, *anything.*"

Her wide eyes made him remember the things they'd done in bed in Vegas, things he'd worked hard to forget.

"You're sure about that?" he said, smiling with false geniality. His gaze raked her again as he pretended to consider her offer. "Anything?"

She whitened. He was pretty sure she was remembering the same erotic caresses they'd shared in Vegas that he was.

Her lips quivering, she stared mutinously at his large body and then the big chrome bed. "I'm sure."

"Forget it," he growled. "I was out of line."

She closed her eyes and took a deep breath. "Thank you." Her long-lashed gaze darted to the stairs behind him.

"I need to check on Taylor again," she said.

"I told you on the plane that when I had my people prepare the nursery they installed a monitor in the baby's room, as well as in the master bedroom. Taylor hasn't made a sound. You said she slept all night."

"A monitor is not the same as a parent."

"She's fine."

"You're probably right, but it's just something that I always do."

"Because you live alone."

"She's in a strange house and bed. I have to make sure she's okay. Please."

The anxiety in her eyes got to him. Deep down, no matter how angry he might be, he'd always wanted to make her feel safe. Besides, he wanted to look in on Taylor, too.

"Okay. But we'll both go," he said.

Taylor was sound asleep, just as he'd known she would be. Still, when Anna insisted on standing by her bed for a few minutes just to make sure, he stood beside her, too, liking her sweet smile and tender expression as she patted their child lovingly. He wished she didn't smell so good.

Hell.

Losing Linda had hurt so badly, he'd avoided women. Until Anna. Then he'd lost his head, crossed a few too many lines, and things had spun crazily out of control.

"I told you she was fine," he said, his voice rough, even as he gently pulled Taylor's blanket higher.

"But she's so little."

"Yes, she is. That's why babies have two parents to protect them. You're not alone anymore. Maybe soon you'll realize that you have nothing to fear here."

"Nothing except you," she said, her eyes burning him in the moonlit darkness.

"Right." Infuriated again, he grabbed her hand and yanked her out the door toward their own bedroom. "What makes you so sure I'll hurt you?" he muttered.

"Today you tracked me down and forced me to come here."

"If I hadn't come, Leo would have sent a stranger. Would you have preferred that, dammit?"

"I would have preferred anyone to you!"

He felt bleak and cold as they walked down the floating stairs to his bedroom again. This time she led while he followed silently.

She was inside their bedroom, moving toward her suitcase, when his cell phone rang.

"Excuse me," he said. He grabbed it and saw Leo's name lit up on the LED.

"Sorry, I've got to take this," Connor said, turning away from her to accept the call.

"But it's so late. Who would be calling you at this hour?"

"Leo, give me a second." Connor covered the mouthpiece and looked up at her again. "It's my brother. Why don't you get undressed and take a shower?"

"While you watch?"

She stood close enough for him to inhale the light, floral scent of her perfume and her shampoo.

"What if I do? We're married."

Giving him a chilling glance, she turned away. Wearily, he sank down on the bed.

"Do you have her?" Leo demanded.

"Yes."

"What have you told her so far?"

"Not much. My showing up was enough of a shock for one day. For both of us."

Connor was aware of Anna moving slowly on the other side of the bedroom, pausing, listening.

"Abby's dying to see her. When can we get together?"

"How about tomorrow afternoon?"

"Terence can't get here so fast, of course. But I'll try to call him after we hang up."

Terence was Becky and Abby's prize-winning journalist father. *Their adoptive father.* But the story was more complicated than that. The girls were the love children of one of the most famous men in Texas, the late Caesar Kemble. Until recently he'd run the Golden Spurs ranch. Their biological mother was Electra Scott, the world famous photojournalist. She was dead, as well. So was their adoptive mother.

Leo said goodbye.

"What did he want?" Anna whispered.

"Like I said, Leo works for your family. They want to meet you. I told him we'd get together tomorrow afternoon."

"My family?" Her hand trembled as she lifted her make-up pouch out of her suitcase, but she didn't press him. He almost wished she had.

"It's pretty complicated. We'll talk about it tomorrow. After breakfast and a few cups of coffee."

She let out a shallow breath.

He smiled. She didn't.

"I don't know about you, but I could use a shower. But ladies first," he growled. Crossing the room, he put his hand on the back of her waist and pushed her in the direction of the master bath. For a long minute he remained frozen, watching the gentle sway of her tantalizing hips while he ground his teeth so hard his jaw hurt.

Living on such intimate terms with her was a bad idea.

She stopped at the stairs that led down to the smaller chamber that had mostly glass walls.

"Drapes? Shades? Neighbors?" she asked, her voice tremulous again as she stared at the dark trees outside.

"The bath looks out on a completely private part of my garden," he said before stomping down the stairs in front of her to show her the various fixtures and how they worked.

"First, you walk down those marble steps. When you

turn on these faucets, water will fall from the ceiling like rain. Most people are impressed, and the design won an award in its day." He ripped two towels off rods and handed them to her.

"Are you going to force me to strip for you, or will you allow me some privacy?"

"You're my wife," he said. "You choose."

"Then go," she whispered.

Six

Big surprise. She hadn't chosen him.

Big surprise—she'd stayed in the shower forever, too—probably to recover from the stunt he'd pulled and to avoid the hell out of him and their marriage bed.

Since he couldn't have Anna, he'd checked on Taylor and had then tossed down a couple of glasses of Scotch before gloomily climbing into bed to wait for Anna.

Liquor was such a lousy consolation prize. By the time she came out of the bathroom wearing his flannel robe, which was so long it trailed behind her on his stone floor, his mood was worse than ever.

"Taylor's fine," he said. "I looked in on her." He'd kissed her warm brow, too.

"You did?" Anna's eyes lit with surprise and gratitude as she unwound the towel that covered her damp hair and dropped it on the floor. Had she thought he'd be an awful, uncaring father?

At the sight of her wet, tousled hair framing her face, his selfish male mind turned to sex again, and he wondered if she was naked underneath his robe. Not that he was likely to find out. When she got into bed, she shot him a worried glance and clutched the lapels over her breasts tighter.

"Good night," he said curtly. "Like I said earlier—I'm not in the mood."

She gave him a look that said she didn't trust him. For once they were on the same page. He didn't trust himself, either.

"Sleep tight," he ground out, even as the sweet floral scents of her soap and shampoo made his body harden.

She nodded in his direction. Frowning, she pressed the bridge of her nose with slim fingertips before yanking the chain to turn off the bedside light.

So much for his dreams of connubial bliss.

He turned out his light, too, and rolled over. Not that he could sleep. Not with her soft, warm body lying so close to his in the moonlit darkness and his male mind imagining her naked and writhing underneath him. Hours later he was still watching glimmers of light and shadow play across the ceiling when Anna cried out and reached for him.

A jolt of pure fire shot through him. Forgetting his anger and frustration, he pulled her closer, suffering an instant erection when her silky warmth enveloped him. "Baby, it's okay."

Unaware of his soothing words and comforting arms, she whimpered like a frightened child while he stared down at her tangled blond hair swirling sweetly across his chest, at the rise and fall of her breasts beneath an extra-large white T-shirt.

At some point she must have tossed his robe on the floor. All she wore was her T-shirt and a pair of panties.

She'd had a few nightmares in Vegas. A couple of nights he'd held her all night long. As in Vegas he wanted to brush her hair back, to stroke her long neck, to kiss her lips. She'd been through too much and had set up her life so that she had no one to rely on but herself. He knew from experience what a lonely, hellish kind of existence that could be. Still, even in his darkest hours, he'd had Leo. Despite the loss of his wife and their unborn child, he'd had his career and ranch and darling little nephew, Caesar. Who had she ever had?

Besides the child she'd stolen from him? he reminded himself angrily. As she slept, the pitiful little sounds she made tore at his heart. Although she wasn't resting peacefully, she wasn't having one of her full-blown nightmares.

Cradling her closer, Connor was increasingly becoming too conscious of her slim, lithe body and its sweet, womanly warmth. As always, his skin flamed, and his body tensed. He swallowed and tried to keep his breathing even so she wouldn't wake up and realize how much he still desired her.

How long he sat there, holding her in his arms, he didn't know. He only knew it was bittersweet.

He closed his eyes and forced himself to count sheep. He was on his fourteenth when she screamed.

"Anna, baby, it's okay. You're with me, Connor."

She shuddered.

"Hey, it's okay."

Suddenly she opened her eyes and saw him looming over her in the darkness. Going rigid, she began to yell and push him away. "What are you doing on my side of the bed? Don't touch me!"

Technically she was on his side of the bed, but he wasn't stupid enough to argue.

"You were having a bad dream."

"It's no concern of yours."

"Right." He held up his hands in mock surrender. "Truce, okay?"

Silence settled over them both for a long minute. Glaring at him, she scooted to her own side of the bed and brushed her hair back from her eyes. "Sorry about that," she said. "I didn't realize…where I was."

"It's okay. I didn't mind."

"Why doesn't that surprise me?"

"Hey, I didn't do anything to you."

"Maybe not this time."

He didn't like remembering how he'd messed things up in Vegas. If he'd been more forthcoming, maybe she would have behaved more rationally. Maybe she would have trusted him a little. Maybe she would have wanted to meet her family.

His determination to do whatever it took to bring her home to Leo, coupled with his fierce attraction to her, had gotten the best of his judgment. He'd seduced her. He'd even married her. He never should have married her without telling her the truth.

Her big eyes were waiflike in the charcoal half-light. Despite her distrust, he wanted to pull her close again, to run his fingers through the silken masses of her blond hair again, to press his lips against the pulse in her throat, to make her feel safe. But she was afraid of him. Could he blame her?

Okay, so he'd tried to take shortcuts and had been less than honest. Still, he wasn't another Dwight. Somehow he had to convince her of that.

"So what was after you this time?" he asked.

She was silent so long, he began to fear he was the villain in her nightmare.

"Bears," she finally admitted.

He fought to conceal his sigh of relief. "How many?"

"Five or six. Giant bears. I was in the woods. Running in the dark. I couldn't really see them. I just knew they were there."

"Where were you running?"

"I was trying to get back... Oh, I don't know. I was lost. Suddenly I could see this light and a tall, white wall. A gate opened and the most beautiful woman dressed all in white held out her hands. But no matter how fast I tried to run, I seemed to stand still. So, she was always out of reach."

"Everybody has dreams like that. Go back to sleep. You're safe."

She stared into his eyes. "Am I?"

He refused to take the bait. "No bears. I swear."

"I know you've got the monitor, but do you think we can go make sure Taylor's okay again?"

"Sure," he said.

When she got up, he followed her, but since Taylor was still sleeping as peacefully as ever they quickly returned, each sliding into his own side of the bed. Knowing how she felt about him, he rolled on his side, turning his broad back to her.

He expected silence.

"Connor?"

"Mmmmm?"

"You were holding me on your side of the bed. You were being nice. I—I'm sorry I was so rude."

"It's okay. I understand. Go to sleep," he muttered.

"But…"

The sheets rustled, and he felt her warmth again as she slid closer. For a long moment she was still, but she was so near, he could feel her breath on his skin. What was her game now?

Tensing, he waited, consumed by his need for her. When she splayed burning fingertips on his back, he stiffened. Then she began moving them round and round in tight little circles, causing every nerve to tighten. Surely she wouldn't be touching him if she didn't want… But hell, who knew?

"You said your brother works for my family, that they had been the one looking for me," she whispered.

"Can't this wait until morning?"

"I can't stop thinking about that dream."

"It was like all your other nightmares, wasn't it? Only maybe not quite as scary?"

"Yes, maybe because you were here."

Finally, she'd said something nice.

"I don't remember anything about having a family… nothing before I was eight or nine. I've always wondered why. Does my family know what happened to me?"

"Tomorrow," he muttered. "Like I said, all that's way too complicated to discuss now."

"My first memory was of the tall, white walls at St. Christopher's Retreat. I had blood on my clothes and a big gash on my arm that the nuns bandaged after Sister Kate found me. I think maybe I thought something terrible was after me. I don't know what. It's all fuzzy now."

"Bears?"

"I don't see how it could have been bears. St. Christopher's was in southern Louisiana. The pioneers killed most all the bears a long time ago."

"Louisiana?" he mumbled sleepily.

"I grew up there. I must have been around eight years old the night I showed up so terrified during a storm. The nuns, with the help of Catholic charities, tried to locate my family and then tried to find me a family to live with. None of the foster families could ever deal with my shyness or nightmares, so Sister Kate always took me back. In between the foster families, I rode the bus to a school about ten miles from the retreat. All the other kids had mothers and daddies and brothers and sisters, and all I had was Sister Kate and Father Kellick and the other nuns. The other kids told me my parents must have been bad."

"Did you believe them?"

"Sort of. But mostly I didn't think about it. I didn't want to. I felt safe at the retreat, and that was enough. School kept me busy."

"What happened to Sister Kate?"

"She died right after I graduated from high school. Heart attack. I found her in her garden lying in her okra. She'd always been such a tower of strength. Suddenly I felt like all my props had been knocked out from under me. From that night on my nightmares started getting worse.

I would wake up screaming, sure someone was right there about to grab me and take me away. I took a job in Montana shortly after Sister Kate's funeral because I wanted to get as far from Louisiana as possible."

"And since then you've had no one?"

She didn't answer for a long time. "Until Dwight, who was my first boss, I…I never let myself get too attached to anybody, especially people I might care for. I saw a psychologist a while back, and she suggested I was afraid of losing them. I never really belonged at the prayer retreat, either. I made too much noise. I couldn't sit still during Mass. I wasn't all that spiritual, so I felt this huge distance between me and everybody else…except Sister Kate. She was tolerant of my shortcomings. 'We all have our vocation,' she would say. 'You'll find yours.'"

"You never had a best friend in school?"

"Once I had a friend over…but you weren't supposed to talk at the prayer retreat or bother the nuns or go near the guests in their guest cottages. My friend and I peeped into one of the cottages, and the guest reported us. My friend made up stories about what happened to her at the retreat, and there was an investigation. After that, I couldn't have a friend over again. So, I just had the stray dogs and cats Sister Kate let me care for. Except for Sister Kate, the nuns kept mostly to themselves, so I sort of got used to doing that myself. I'm pretty self-reliant."

"Still, you must have been lonely at times," he said. He could definitely identify.

Nestling against him, her mouth accidentally brushed his shoulder blades as she shaped herself against his body. Suddenly every nerve in his body was entirely focused on her.

Bending her knees, she fitted herself against him so that they lay together as they had in Vegas after making love. But this wasn't Vegas.

"I was so scared of those bears…so glad you…" She ran a fingertip along the elastic waistband of his pajama bottoms.

"What are you doing? You're the girl who can't get close to anybody, remember?"

When the fingertip slid beneath his waistband, he threw off the sheet and sprang out of bed. "Look, there's only so much a guy can stand."

He was hot and hard and fully aroused, which was a problem, since she didn't want him. Maybe he'd forced her to come here, but there were lines he wouldn't cross. He didn't like being played for a sucker, either.

He tore across the bedroom to the bathroom where he stripped off his pajama bottoms and walked into the sunken shower. He turned on the jets full blast so that icy water rained from the ceiling. Panting, he leaned against the icy tile walls and let the cold water pour over him.

"Connor…"

He jerked toward the sound of her voice, water flying from his head. "Leave me alone."

He was aware of her light footsteps in the bathroom. Moonlight streamed through the tall glass windows. Bathed in the silver light, gloriously naked, she stepped onto the top step and adjusted the taps that made the water heat.

"Damn it, go back to bed," he whispered even as his eyes remained fastened on the delectable swells of her breasts and hips.

"Can't sleep," she replied. Her low voice sent an unwanted trill of excitement through him as his gaze drifted to her thighs.

"Don't want to," she added. Meeting his gaze, she walked down the stairs and joined him in the steamy mists.

This is a power play. Don't fall for it.

She stepped into the falling warm water and threw back her head so that the sparkling water streamed over her. Her body seemed aglow. She looked like an ethereal water nymph beneath a spray of diamonds.

Hell, it had been too long. He was such a sap. He wanted her with every cell in his being…he never stood a chance.

"Go back to bed unless you want—"

"I know you lied to me, but God help me I want—"

On a savage groan, he opened his arms, and she flew into them. He crushed her slick, wet body against his. Recklessly he slid his hands up her long, graceful neck and cupped her delicate chin. Their gazes locked. They didn't speak, at least not in words, but the hot, torrid conflict raging in her eyes equaled his.

For more than a year and a half she'd run from him. Who knew why she was doing this now? At this hour he was past caring.

"Wrap your legs around me," he whispered.

She jumped, and he caught her. Her heart was pounding as violently as his. Maybe she'd hate him again tomorrow. Maybe not. All he knew for sure was that she was as hot for him as he was for her.

When his manhood probed against her softest, most secret tissues, she gasped.

"Why did you lie to me, Connor?"

Later. He pressed a fingertip to her lips. "Don't spoil it."

Next he lowered his mouth to hers and kissed her deeply. Her lips parted greedily. Open mouth to open mouth, they tasted each other.

Surrendering, she accepted more of his tongue and then gave him hers. Closing his eyes, he pulled her even closer. Their kiss deepened, growing hotter and hotter even as he grew harder and needier.

Whirling her around, he slammed her against the wet, tall wall and fused his taut, aroused body to hers so that they stood, his sex against hers.

She gasped at the intimacy.

"Are you sure about this?" he whispered as water streamed over them. "No games?"

When she nodded, he closed his eyes and prayed he'd heard correctly.

"Please," she whispered, arching toward him. "Please…"

His heart racing, he drove inside her.

She was tight, wet and satiny warm—pure, exquisite bliss. Ever since she'd run, he'd missed her, craved this. Again and again he plunged, soaring as his pleasure built.

In the shimmering gray light with the water falling on them like rain, their urgent, writhing bodies spoke a language that was infinitely sweet and pure. In those brief moments, neither her hate nor her fear nor his anger separated them. She clung, whispering heated love words against his ear. He felt that she belonged to him completely, that she gave of herself freely, wholly. No matter what she'd done, he never wanted to let her go.

"Anna…Anna…Becky… Baby, be mine…." He was speaking so low and breathing so heavily, his words were barely audible. "I'll keep you safe, I swear."

Then she sank to her knees and took him into her mouth, kissing him lovingly and expertly until he exploded.

Later, when she stood up, he kissed her softly on her mouth, on her radiant cheeks, on her silken throat. She nuzzled her cheek against his. Silently he lifted her into his arms and carried her out of the shower to their bed. She did not scoot to her own side as before, but lay nestled against him trustingly, adoringly.

"Don't be afraid of the bears," he whispered.

She laughed. "They wouldn't dare come back with you here."

He kissed her throat, caressed her hair. "This time will be for you."

He made love to her again and again. In the bed. On the floor. On the floating staircase. Afterward, sated, he gathered her close and took her back to bed, where he slept long and deeply wrapped in her arms.

He was still angry that she'd kept Taylor from him. They still had a lot of unresolved issues. He didn't like the feeling he was getting in too deep, too fast, but her warmth and sweetness intoxicated him.

He didn't fight his drowsiness. Tomorrow would be soon enough to tackle their problems and worry about the future.

Seven

Anna blinked against the sparkling sunlight. When she realized her arms and legs were deliciously entwined around Connor's warm body, she smiled shyly, a soft peacefulness wrapping her. His warmth made her almost too lazy to care about this mysterious family she had to meet today.

She'd never liked meeting new people, but she shoved that to the back of her mind. It was much more pleasant to let her gaze drift from his tousled blond hair to his wide, naked chest and flat, muscular stomach.

He was sleek and tanned—too gorgeous for words. At first she almost thought she was in Vegas again during those first blissful, winter days and nights when she'd been so infuriated with him—before she'd known who and what he was: a liar.

Only slowly, as her eyes left him and she focused on the hot sunlight dissolving into dancing shadows on his tall walls, and she began to listen to the screech of cicadas outside, did she remember where she was. Connor, who would be furious at her again when he woke up, had all but made her his prisoner in his gorgeous mansion.

How could she have seduced him last night after what he'd done? Answer: because her dream had made her feel lonely and vulnerable. Because his warmth and strength had always made her feel so protected. Because lying beside him had awakened memories of Vegas and what she'd hoped for.

Last night, wrapped in his arms afterward, she'd felt so safe. For the first time in her life, she'd felt that she belonged to someone who would take care of her. It hadn't mattered that Vegas had been a ridiculous fantasy, that he'd been paid to find her or that their marriage had been based on his lies and her stupidity.

Her concerns made her heart beat faster. Shifting out of his embrace, she studied his dark, carved face. Asleep, all the tension and anger were gone from his determined features. So was the hot, possessive sexuality that had blazed in his eyes when he'd shoved her against the shower wall right before he'd plunged inside her, claiming her as he might a war prize.

Even now, as she slid away from him to her own side of the bed, she felt the old, awful loneliness creeping over her, and instantly she got a crazy rush at the thought of snuggling against him again. But would that really erase the harsh realities of her existence?

She'd felt so alone and lost when she'd learned she was

pregnant. Her mind had gone over everything he'd said, everything he'd done. She'd wanted to hate him totally, but part of her had known unbearable pain because she'd believed she'd never hear his voice again or see him again.

Now he was back. He'd made love to her. And that had been wonderful.

For a long time Anna lay there, letting the past and all the memories of her mistakes wash over her. Would she ever get her life on track?

Finally she crept out of the bed, stopping only to pull on his robe. She climbed the floating stairs. First, of course, she had to check on Taylor.

Taylor's body was curled up in her blanket. She looked as happy as a contented kitten in her pretty new bed in her daddy's house.

Once Anna had made sure her precious baby was still sleeping soundly, she was too curious about Connor not to explore his house while she had the chance.

Swiftly, afraid he'd awaken soon, she wandered from room to room. The master bedroom was on the lower floor. The other bedrooms and the main rooms of his home were on the middle level of the three-story home.

In the closet of the guest bedroom next to Taylor's, she found the beautiful clothes he'd bought her in Vegas arranged neatly on wooden hangers. For a long moment she buried her face in the soft fox fur coat, remembering how she'd loved wearing it when they'd gone out. She'd felt so elegant in her strapless wedding gown and that fur.

When she saw a cardboard box on the floor marked *Becky,* she knelt and folded the brown flaps back, only to gasp when she saw all the precious little souvenirs she'd collected during those two wonderful weeks when they'd been together. Why had he saved everything?

With a shaking hand she touched the matchbooks from the restaurants where they'd dined, the champagne glasses they'd sipped from the first night he'd made love to her, the two tour books about the Hoover Dam and Death Valley she'd bought and read after their tour and hike. Finally, on the bottom of the box, her fingertips touched something soft.

Holding her breath, she lifted two black velvet boxes. Opening them, she bit her lip when she saw all three of their rings—her two and his.

Her diamond engagement ring was brilliant in the sunlight. Remembering how thrilled she'd been with her rings, how often she'd held up her hand to glance at them, her stomach tightened. When he'd slid those rings on her finger, she'd never been happier. She'd felt brave and strong enough to face anything.

How quickly everything had changed.

With a cry, she slammed the boxes shut again and buried them beneath the heavy tour books. Then she stood up and closed the closet doors. For a long moment she just stood there.

Breathing fast and sniffling a little despite her determination not to cry, she resumed her tour with a vengeance. With its tall windows, its white, sun-splashed walls, its supermodern design, its lovely, minimalist furnishings, and its private grounds, his house was like a fairy-tale palace in a dream. She'd never really had a home, and she liked it far too much, even though she knew it was dangerous to like anything when she and Taylor couldn't possibly stay. Still, behind the tall walls that surrounded the back part of the house, a little girl could play without being observed by strangers driving past on the street. She imagined a swing set and a playhouse before she stopped herself from daydreaming.

They weren't staying, and that was that. She was trying to find things out about him, not fall in love with his house.

Quickly, she walked into his kitchen and opened his fridge. Except for three six-packs of Mexican beer, a dozen eggs, coffee and a pound of bacon, all she saw was gleaming white plastic-and-glass shelves. Obviously, he was no cook. There wasn't a single piece of fruit, either.

From kitchen to dining room to living room, his furnishings were simple and modern, his paintings bright, geometric designs that revealed nothing about their owner.

All the main rooms on the middle floor were so dust-free and amazingly neat, she was sure he had a maid. His office, which was on the third floor, was a different story.

When she opened the blinds beside his desk, they revealed a view of his front yard and its green lawns sloping down to the wide street. Like the lower floors of his house, the grounds were perfectly kept. He must have a gardener, too. Which made sense, since he'd told her he worked all the time and was gone a lot.

Dozens of papers, file folders, envelopes and sticky notes fought for space on his crowded desk. Clearly no maid trespassed in here.

Family photographs filled one shelf on the wall. There was a faded snapshot of two little boys in Stetsons and jeans astride huge horses. Or did the horses just look so large because the boys were so small? When she recognized Connor by the stubborn set of his jaw, she was nearly sure the older, taller, darker kid with the identical jawline had to be his big brother, Leo. A second black-and-white picture with curling edges was of the two brothers and a plump, plainly dressed woman, probably their mother.

Why did old photographs always make her so aware of loss?

The next picture took her breath away.

Her hands trembled as she lifted the colored eight-by-ten of a blond woman, a black-haired man and their dark-haired toddler, who closely resembled his father. All three wore matching black cowboy hats and shirts.

Anna stared at the woman. Involuntarily, she traced her features with a fingertip.

The woman looked exactly like her.

Staring into the woman's hazel eyes that slanted in the exact same way her own did, Anna swallowed against the sudden tightness in her throat. Her fingers clenched around the picture frame. She felt haunted, lost, and yet excited too.

Who was this woman who looked so happy and trusting, this woman who drew her as no one else ever had, who almost seemed a part of her?

They had to be related.

An image of two little girls with blond braids dressed in identical red shorts and white shirts, laughing as they ran after a wild turkey in the desert, flashed in Anna's mind. As quickly as it came, the elusive vision was gone.

Feeling shaky and a little dizzy, Anna squeezed her lashes shut and then pressed a fingertip to her temple as she tried to think, feel or remember more than that fragment, anything about her forgotten past. But her mind was the same awful blank it had always been.

She stared at the photograph. The woman appeared to be her own age. Were they sisters? Twins?

Again she saw the two little girls with braids. Only this time they were riding a horse bareback together.

The picture in Connor's book in Vegas.

Somehow she knew her flashback wasn't about that picture. It was a long-forgotten memory. One of those little girls on the horse was her.

Anna's heart pumped wildly. If this woman was her sister, how could she have forgotten her? Was there some terrifying reason she'd chosen to forget the first few years of her life? What had happened to her, to her family? Why had she been wandering in those woods outside St. Christopher's?

She remembered Connor's quote on his Web page. "I can't always give everybody a happy ending, but I can usually give them the truth. From there a person can…rebuild."

The truth. Anna began to tremble. Who was she?

Becky. Connor had called her Becky in the airport and then again after he'd made love to her on their wedding night. Was that really her name?

Slowly, she set the photograph back in its place. When she turned away, her eyes lit on a thick file in the middle of Connor's desk. Bold black letters scribbled across it spelled out the name Rebecca Collins.

The hair on the back of Anna's neck rose as she read and reread the name.

Rebecca Collins.

Becky. The name triggered strange, fragile emotions that she couldn't seem to hold on to.

Too dazed to think, Anna sank into Connor's chair behind the desk and opened the file. Most of the pages were dog-eared. Wondering if he'd poured over the pages, searching for clues that might lead him to her, she flipped through them until she came to a report with the title Abigail Collins Storm. A tattered snapshot exactly like the framed one on his shelf was stapled at a crazy angle in the top right-hand corner of the document.

"Abigail," Anna whispered.

"Abby! *Abby!*" The name and its nickname registered on some deep level just as the name Becky had.

Curious, Anna began to read. His summary and the date on the first page told her that Connor had interviewed Abigail in her Austin office about her twin's disappearnce not long before he'd shown up at the Albuquerque airport.

Abby's twin?

That would be me.

Anna's gaze flew back to the photograph. Again, the startling resemblance made her mouth go dry. Connor had said he was working for her family. Clearly, he'd been telling the truth about something.

With a shiver, she lowered her head over the folder and began to read what Abby had said.

You don't know how important little sequences of ordinary events are until…until something horrible happens, like losing your twin sister, and you keep going over them again and again as I have. For years.

It was all my fault…Becky disappearing. Our family was never the same. And all because of me. If only… But you don't want feelings. You want facts.

We were eight. We'd gotten into trouble for being too noisy in the tent. We were camping in the Franklin Mountains in El Paso with our parents, you see. And we were shooed out of the tent to play chase and hide-and-seek. When we spotted a wild turkey spreading his tail feathers, we ran after him. That's how we got so far from the campground so fast. Then the sun began to go down, and I realized we were alone. I told Becky we had to go back. But Becky wanted to chase the turkey. I should have made her stop. I left her out there alone….

Abigail's guilt-stricken words made Anna's heart quicken. Not that she remembered Abigail or the turkey, really. Her earliest memories were of those tall, white walls surrounding St. Christopher's and Sister Kate. Before them—nothing.

The photographs inside the folder of two identical little blond girls in braids brought tears. Coupled with Abigail's interview, those pictures touched her so profoundly, Anna had to stop reading.

Suddenly it was all too much. Pitching the pictures back inside, she slammed the folder shut. Then she buried her face in her hands.

Her family wanted to meet her, but how could she face any of them when they were strangers? She needed time.

* * *

When Connor woke up, Anna's pillow was empty, and the silent house felt heavy and oppressive. Except for the screeching sounds of the cicadas outside, nothing stirred.

He remembered their wedding night in Vegas, when she'd run out on him. Was he alone in the house? Had she left him and taken Taylor?

As he sprang out of bed, flashes of hot, white sunlight splashed the far wall and ceiling. Logically he knew that if she opened a door or a window, his alarm would have gone off.

Grabbing his jeans, he bolted up the stairs to Taylor's room. The baby was still asleep, but making faint mewing sounds, like she might wake up sometime soon.

Her back to him, Anna stood at the window, still wearing his long flannel robe that swallowed her. Her stance was that of a caged animal yearning for its freedom as she clutched the drape with tensed fingers and peered outside. Has she been crying? Because she thought he'd taken advantage of her last night? Hell, had he?

Not that her tears or regrets could matter. He had to tell her about Abby and Leo and Terence. About Electra and Joanne and the Golden Spurs Ranch. It was all so complicated. Then she had to meet whichever family members showed up today. Taylor, too. Too much for their first day home, probably. But necessary. Abby had been waiting a long time for this day.

"You okay?" he asked as he pulled on his jeans.

She whirled. Her eyes were red, her cheeks tear-streaked. "Do you even own a ranch? Was everything you told me in Vegas a lie?"

He stiffened and then forced an answer. "Yeah. I have a ranch. The Little Spur. Or at least half of it. My brother owns the other half. It's near Bastrop. Which is near Austin."

"But mostly you're a P.I.?"

"Mostly. I got into this line of work after the military. But I grew up on a ranch. Does that count?"

Instead of smiling at his weak attempt at humor, she swallowed. "You've told so many lies, I don't know what to believe."

"Right. I'm to blame for everything that's wrong in our relationship. I don't usually take cases like this anymore, but before I went into business for myself, I worked as a professional investigator for a friend, a P.I. His specialty was kidnapped kids and missing persons. He taught me everything he knew. I developed a reputation. Bottom line— I'm good at finding people like you."

"Why me? What happened to me?"

"You were kidnapped."

"By whom?" she whispered, sinking against the rails of the crib.

"Until six months ago, nobody knew. They got away. A white van was found off Interstate 10 near Beaumont, Texas, with half of a blood-smeared ransom note inside it. *Your blood.* There'd been a struggle, maybe among the kidnappers themselves. You were gone. My agent found the police records on that van and ran the DNA and matched it to Abby…and therefore to you. But that was twenty years after the fact. Then a couple of months ago, two guys serving life sentences in La Mesa Prison in Tijuana confessed to the kidnapping. They worked for the Morales Drug Cartel, whose leaders had a grudge against your father, who was a journalist. Your father had written in-criminating articles about the Morales Cartel. I guess the good news is, at least, you know your kidnappers are behind bars and present no danger to you."

"At least..."

Connor finger-combed his heavy hair. "My brother, who's the CEO of the Golden Spurs Ranch, paid me to find you. His boss, Joanne Kemble, is the widow of the late Caesar Kemble. Your biological father was the rancher—not the journalist who adopted you because Caesar didn't want his wife to know he'd cheated on her.

"The Kembles have owned the Golden Spurs for well over a century. Joanne lives on the ranch and runs the cattle operation. Not too long ago she finally did discover that Caesar had indeed betrayed her and had conceived two daughters, twins, whom he never told her about—you and Abby. She told Leo to find Caesar's secret daughters, so Leo hired me. I found Abigail first. Leo married her. They have a kid. Little Caesar."

She blinked.

"Sorry. That was probably way too much information."

She nodded.

"I saw Abby's picture," Anna breathed, her eyes wide. "Along with pictures of two little girls who looked just like me when I showed up at St. Christopher's. Why couldn't they have found me back then?"

"People tried. But the cops who had jurisdiction were in El Paso. They thought you'd been taken to Mexico. There was a storm or two in Louisiana. Records were lost. Nobody connected the dots."

"And a little girl was out there all those years...lost. *Me.*"

"She doesn't have to be. Not anymore," he said. "You have a family who wants to meet you."

"It's not that easy," she whispered.

He strode to the crib and took her in his arms. "Maybe it could be."

Tentatively her hands crawled up his chest and circled his neck. His grip tightened, and she clung while he rocked her back and forth.

Then Taylor started fisting her hands and jamming them into her mouth before letting out a yelp.

"This conversation is adjourned for now," he said, kissing Anna on the tip of her nose before releasing her. Smiling down at Taylor, he whispered, "Little tyrant."

Anna turned to their daughter, as well. "Thank you for telling me about my family," she murmured to Connor.

When she lifted Taylor into her arms and held her close, Taylor smiled.

"My family doesn't feel real to me. Only Taylor seems real." Anna brushed the baby's nose with a gentle fingertip.

"That will change in time," he said.

"Will it?" she whispered, her worried eyes meeting his. "Do you really think it will be that easy?"

Eight

How to deal with Anna?

Seated behind his desk in his shadowy third-floor office, Connor seethed with concern as he stared out at his well-manicured lawn, which sloped down to the sidewalk. Across the street, a little redheaded boy was riding a shiny blue tricycle under the watchful gaze of his mother.

Connor knew his neighbors only slightly, but he'd seen the way the woman and her husband looked at each other at block parties, the way one of the parents was always with the boy.

If he wanted Taylor in his life full-time, he had to deal with Anna. He didn't like the way she'd avoided him ever since he'd told her about her family.

Hell. He couldn't think. Maybe if he went for a run, breathed some fresh air, he could sort his thoughts out.

He drummed his hand on his desk for a long minute. Then he grabbed his phone and asked Sam Guerra, his top investigator, to come over and keep an eye on Anna and Taylor while he was out.

When Connor returned from his run that included buying a kiddie swing at a yard sale, he was no closer to an answer than before he'd left. He was on his way to the back door when he heard Anna in the nursery. She was changing a diaper and singing to Taylor, who cooed along tunelessly. He stopped outside the nursery. Lurking in the doorway, out of sight, he almost started whistling along. Holding on to the kiddie swing and lengths of chain, his heart knocked at a crazy beat. He couldn't let Taylor go.

For a long moment his gaze devoured Anna's slim back. Despite her faded, baggy jeans and the old yellow sweater, he had no difficulty imagining the sleek, sexy body he'd ravished in his shower last night. Still, he needed to take her shopping for prettier clothes.

Anna… Just the memory of what she'd done to him against that wet wall, when she'd knelt before him and taken him in her satiny mouth, made him ache for more of the same. His heart rushed violently, and he got rock hard.

Not that she looked the wanton this morning, with her gleaming, dark blond hair tied back with a ribbon. No, she looked as demure and innocent as a schoolgirl.

He thought about all that she might have been through, about the difficulty she had making friends, about Dwight stalking her. Connor's misrepresenting himself for those two whole weeks in Vegas had aggravated the situation. It was too easy to understand why she didn't trust him.

So, what the hell could he do about any of it? He didn't see an easy fix. All he knew was that he wasn't about to let her go.

He must have made some sound—maybe the chains rattled—because she sensed him and turned. Arching a brow, she colored. "Did you have to hire that same goon, the one who showed up in Santa Fe, to make sure I didn't run?"

"Sam's my number-one investigator. You should be flattered that I value you so highly."

"No arguments then that I'm your prisoner?"

"Was that what last night was about? Winning my confidence, so I'd do something stupid…like leave you on your own this morning so you could take our baby and leave me?"

"You set the alarm and dead bolts. I don't have a key or the code."

"So glad you noticed."

She glared at him. "You made quite a point of it."

He forced a smile. "You could still open the door and run. By the time anybody got here, you'd have a helluva head start."

"You read me like a book." She clapped her hands. "Did you make all As in detective school?"

With immense difficulty Connor checked his temper.

"Look, Sam wasn't just watching you for me. He was here to protect you and Taylor while I was gone. I didn't want you to worry about any of those bears in your nightmares getting you or Taylor. Or Dwight." His deep voice softened. "I want you to feel safe here."

"Oh."

"I want to keep you safe so you'll stay…and Taylor will stay."

"You know that's impossible."

"Reconcile yourself to it, Anna," he said as gently and as patiently as he could. "I mean to keep Taylor near me…and that means I want you, too."

"For how long?"

"I don't know yet."

She opened her mouth as if to protest, then stopped.

"While I was out running, I called Leo. He's bringing Abby and Caesar at two this afternoon. Joanne Kemble's going to try to make it, as well. She's your stepmother, by the way."

"I…I can't meet them. At least, not today. Please—"

He dropped the swing and chains. In two long strides he spanned the distance that separated them. "You've been through hell. Don't underestimate yourself. You've got way more guts than you give yourself credit for."

"I can't do any of this…you…this sham of a marriage…my family. I won't be forced."

"And I won't be forced, either." He couldn't keep the thick undertone of bitterness out of his clipped tone. "Taylor won't grow up alone the way you did."

"No. She'll have a mother! Me!"

"You're not enough. A single parent is never enough. She needs us both. She needs the rest of her family. You're going to give your family a chance for her sake, whether you want to or not." Damn. He hadn't meant for it to come out that way.

She glared at him for what seemed like an eternity. Even so he sensed overwhelming vulnerability. Maybe that's why he relented.

"Look, I've said too much, too soon. I shouldn't have pushed so hard. Hell, it's nearly ten. I'm starved. Are you hungry?"

She sucked in a breath. Then, much to his surprise, she nodded. "Starved," she admitted.

Maybe she was sick and tired of quarreling, too.

"Then how about a truce while I fix us some breakfast, which happens to be the only meal I know how to cook. If we stick together, you may want to learn to cook."

Again, she put up no argument. "I guessed that might be the case when I saw your kitchen. The beer and eggs and bacon in your refrigerator were a clue. Don't you ever crave a banana?"

"Have you been snooping?"

"Before I went to your office."

The idea of her roaming about his house like she owned the place was going to take some getting used to. But if they were married, she had a right to do so. She'd never settle down if she didn't.

"The house is crying for a woman's touch," he said.

"You have a maid."

"Not the same." He felt an aching tightness in his throat as he remembered how Anna had pleasured him last night in the bathroom.

Her quick blush followed by a frown made him wonder if her mind was running along the same lines.

In the kitchen he scrambled eggs and popped slices of bread into the toaster while she nuked the bacon.

"I'm not much of a cook, either," she admitted. "I usually make a smoothie for breakfast."

He couldn't think of anything to say, and they prepared

the rest of the meal in silence. When they sat down to eat at his chrome kitchen table, except for the clatter of silverware on china, they were silent.

From time to time, she shot glances his way, but when he noticed, she quickly averted her eyes. He straightened his shoulders. Why was being with her so difficult?

When they finished eating, he stacked their plates and glanced at her. She knotted her hands on top of the table, her gaze on the empty plates he held. The day ahead of them suddenly seemed never ending.

"Before we have our meeting, I have to go into the office," he said, his tone low and edgy. He didn't quite trust leaving her at the house by herself, even with Guerra. People who wanted to bolt found a way.

"And Sam Guerra? Will he go, too?"

"He stays."

Her brows flew together.

"To protect you from the bears," he said, striving for a light touch.

"How long do you think we can live like this?" she snapped.

"Like I said, I don't know. You want to know something? I don't like this any better than you do." He pushed his chair back. "But for now—we'll both just have to adjust. I wouldn't be able to get a damn thing done at the office if I was wondering whether you and the baby would still be here when I got back."

"And when you return—then what?"

"*I don't know.* I'm making this up as we go along." He tossed his napkin onto the table. "Hey, relax. I won't be gone long."

"Do you really think I care if you never come back?" she snapped.

Bitter frustration lit a fuse that began to spark. Still, somehow, he managed to contain his temper.

"Looks like despite your friendliness in our shower last night, our marriage is off to a rocky start." He forced a smile. "Which means there's nowhere to go but up."

"Last night wasn't some new beginning. *Our marriage is over.* I told you that a year and a half ago. Why won't you listen?"

"Legally, we're still married, which means you're still my wife."

"What do you want from me?"

"Lots and lots of things. Maybe a little revenge for starters," he said, anger beginning to drive him. "And Taylor. You put me in hell, Anna. Think about that."

She drew in a sharp breath.

"Think about this, too," he said. "You've had over nine months to get to know her. I'd like a chance with her, too. Then there's your family. They have needs, too. When you're part of a family, it can't just be about you anymore, Anna. Other people matter, too."

She went still for a long minute as if his eyes held her spellbound. His gaze lowered to her lips.

"And I wouldn't pass up more of what you offered last night in the shower…should you be in the mood to offer it again."

"I won't!"

"Funny, I got the impression you found me hard to resist last night. *You* seduced *me,* remember?"

"Of all the conceited, arrogant…stupid…"

He cut her off. "I know it's still early, and I shouldn't tempt you…but hell, you look so damn good, maybe I can't help myself."

Hardly knowing what he was about before he seized her by both arms, he yanked her hard against his body.

Why couldn't he stop himself where she was concerned?

She smelled so sweet, and her hair was so soft. When she began twisting to escape him, her hair spilled out of its demure ribbon onto his arms.

"Be still!" His words were halting and raspy because her pelvis was sliding against his thighs.

When she kicked him in the shin, he crushed her more tightly against himself. Winding his hand in her thick hair, he pulled her head back and pressed his mouth to her warm throat.

"You have no idea what you do to me or how much I want you," he muttered thickly. "Or maybe you do." His lips left a trail of erotic kisses along her neck to her shoulders. "I don't want to fight. I want to love you. I want to love you so much."

His arms tightened, drawing her closer. His lips blazed over her nipples. "Baby, you want to know what I'd do if Sam wasn't upstairs listening to everything we're doing and saying—"

"No!" She shook her head wildly.

Sexual tension raced along every nerve ending in his body as he leaned down and took her with him. His tongue swept her ear, licked inside it. Then he whispered in a rough, low tone, "I'd take you right here on the kitchen table, and you'd beg me for more."

"No! I think you're a savage! I hid from you for a year and a half, remember?"

His mouth quirked, but his smile was humorless.

Breathing hard, she raised her hand to slap him, but he was faster.

"Yeah. I remember," he said, wrapping her fingers in his. He kissed her wrists. Then he moved her hands down and pressed them against his straining masculinity. "And I wanted you every damn second you were gone."

Their gazes locked. He could tell that feeling him and knowing how much he wanted her made her cheeks heat. He raised her hand from his thigh and kissed each fingertip again. Then he looked her straight in the eye. "You're heart is beating way too fast for a woman who doesn't want more. Your eyes are on fire. Why is that, I wonder?"

She clenched her fists and pushed against him. He held on and with a final shake, her body shuddered and melted against his.

"I hate what you do to me," she whispered, even as she arched herself against his hips. "I hate being weak like this."

His grip tightening, he pulled her lower body snug against his aroused manhood again, so she couldn't possibly avoid knowing how she affected him. When she didn't try to pull away, he rained kisses on her face, her neck and her shoulder. "You're not weak. I need you, too. What's wrong with that? We're married."

"Not for long."

"All the more reason to make the most it," he murmured, deliberately mocking her.

Her arms went up and closed around his neck, pulling his face closer to hers again.

"You missed me then…at least a little…while you were hiding?" he said.

"No…."

"Well, you damn sure haunted me."

"Every night when I was alone in bed I vowed to hate you," she said.

"Good to know you were thinking about me, too."

"No."

"Look, we have a child. We have to try to make this work for her sake."

"No. It can't work," she whispered, even as she stared at his lips.

"You're right. If you refuse to look at this from a positive angle, it can't. But what if you focused on making it work? Then what?"

"No."

"Why don't you give yourself and us…me…a chance? People can change. Even you. Maybe how you've lived isn't enough anymore. Just because you've lived a certain way doesn't mean you have to go on that way, or even that you can. You're a mother now. Do you want Taylor to become as scared and inhibited as you? *She* wasn't kidnapped, *you* were! Maybe you need to deal with what happened for her sake."

Anna was shaking her head even as she lifted her lips to his, saying no and yet saying yes, too. When she opened her mouth, he took all she wanted to give, kissing her again and again until he felt too close to the edge.

His heart thrummed. Heat coursed through him, and he knew if he didn't stop, he wouldn't be able to resist taking her on his kitchen table for much longer.

"Damn you," he swore as he tore himself loose. "I always lose my head around you."

Nine

True to his word, Connor was gone several hours, which gave Anna time to regroup. She did some laundry and read the newspaper and forced her mind to topics other than him and his kisses.

What a luxury it was to have time to read. As a caregiver, she'd never had a free second in New Orleans. As the wife of a wealthy man, she would have a privileged life. So would Taylor.

Don't think about that.

At the sound of a car in the drive, she stilled. Alert as a cat, she listened to the garage door rumble upward. Then Connor's heavy footsteps resounded downstairs. Were all men so noisy?

Shutting her book that she hadn't really been reading, she raced into Taylor's room where she busied herself straightening all the pink darling clothes she'd washed. Then she put them into drawers.

She held her breath, wondering if he would come looking for her. But instead of seeking her out and kissing her again, he yelled to Sam to join him out in the backyard.

For a while all was quiet. Filled with curiosity and an odd sense of expectancy that made her pulse throb, she waited. And waited. Then the drilling and hammering began.

She ran to the bay window. Connor was way out on a high limb of a pecan tree adjusting chains that he'd attached to the red-and-blue baby swing he'd bought earlier. She caught her breath and watched him anxiously. Not that he didn't seem self-assured and very confident up in that tree.

Beneath him Sam held the little seat at different heights above the ground while Connor shouted commands.

Soon the swing was secure, and she was holding her breath as Connor climbed down, jumping lithely to the ground again. When he stood, his long legs apart, admiring the swing, a faint breeze lifted his heavy, golden hair. He began pushing the swing back and forth while Guerra watched.

Why did Connor have to be so handsome? So sexy? She felt like she was seventeen and infatuated for the first time. She wanted to open the window and yell down to him, and then run out to the yard and join him.

She imagined herself glancing up at him from beneath her lashes, bragging on him for installing the swing. He would smile that easy smile that took her breath away. Maybe he'd take her hand in his, kiss her. Maybe he'd pull her close. And then maybe—

No! With a heartfelt sigh, she squeezed her eyes shut.

She saw him swinging a laughing Taylor on a warm, lazy evening after work while she sipped iced tea in the hammock and watched them. She imagined a lifetime of such evenings. Taylor taller, sitting beside her father as she eagerly stumbled over the first words in a reader; Taylor dying Easter eggs with Anna while Connor watched over the top of his newspaper; Taylor splashing about in the pool, swimming from one parent's arms to the other's.

Anna's eyes snapped open. She had to force herself to end the foolish daydreams. He was a liar, and she was an idiot. She couldn't risk her heart again by thinking about a happy, shared future with Connor Storm.

"Damn him," she whispered, turning away, her eyes hot and wet.

Anna started when she heard Connor's footsteps on the floating stairs. It was a quarter past two. She'd heard the doorbell a few minutes earlier.

"Everybody's here," he said in a quiet, low tone. "Abby, Caesar, Leo…Joanne."

"My stepmother."

"Right. They're in the living room," he said. "I started coffee."

"Give me a minute," Anna whispered, not turning around to face him. Queasy with nerves, she stood before the mirror in their bedroom, applying lipstick, retracing the color over her bottom lip many more times than necessary.

"All right. I'll serve the coffee without you."

She set her lipstick tube on the dresser and then frowned at her too-vivid mouth with distaste. Her skin was such a sickly white, she'd thought she'd needed color, but the garish red only made her look paler. She wiped some of the lipstick off and then slowly turned to mount the floating stairs.

Even from the kitchen she could hear their bright, overly eager voices. They were admiring Taylor and laughing, and Taylor, who loved adoring fans, was cooing responsively.

Anna took a faltering step into the living room and froze. All gaiety died. In its place an embarrassing hush filled the room as too many eyes focused on her. Anna felt conspicuous and shy. Even so she struggled to smile politely.

Joanne—surely the attractive, older redhead had to be her stepmother—rushed forward and clasped her hand.

"Welcome home, dear. We've all waited for this moment for so long." Her face softened. "I spoke to Terence, *your* dear father. He will be here as soon as he can."

Anna pulled her hand free. Vaguely, she saw the scrapbooks and files from Connor's office that lay open on the coffee table. A dark-haired little boy sat beside Abby and Leo, who held Taylor.

"Becky," Abby whispered, her luminous eyes both loving and troubled. "Darling." Her voice was gentle and so sweet, oh so sweet. It sounded like music, once loved, but long-forgotten. *No. Never forgotten.*

That sound had been locked away inside Anna somewhere, and upon hearing it, Anna remembered two little girls, holding hands and skipping; two little girls who'd thought nothing would ever separate them.

She remembered hard hands grabbing her and pitching her into a cargo van. She'd fought them. She'd fought so hard.

How did she know that? All she knew for sure was that she'd been alone in the back of that van, and more or less alone ever since, when once she'd had someone she'd shared everything with.

Without consciously knowing it, Anna took a single backward step. As shy as a child in a roomful of strangers, she felt increasingly awkward.

As if sensing her discomfort, Connor crossed the room in two swift strides, his large, tanned hand reaching out to pull her closer, his fingers warm, but nevertheless, they locked around her wrist like a vise.

The long sleeves of his white shirt were rolled up almost to his elbows. She caught the familiar scent of his cologne. Nothing in his manner seemed alarming. He looked relaxed. Only she knew his hand was a manacle.

Anna straightened. When she felt the pressure of his other hand against the small of her back, she gently pushed him away.

"I'm…I'm afraid I have a headache," she said. "If you'll excuse me…"

She didn't want to make a scene, but she had to get away. They all, even Connor, expected her to be the little girl they'd lost. Walls might be tumbling in her mind, but she barely remembered that little girl. She wasn't even sure she knew herself anymore.

"I'm sorry," Anna whispered. "I really don't feel at all well."

"Let her go," Abby said in that sweet, musical tone that was so familiar. "We can do this later. When she's feeling more rested. Just seeing her and knowing she's safe… alive…playing with Taylor…is enough…for now."

Connor's eyes glinted, whether with silent sympathy or the desire to control her, she didn't know, but he released Anna's hand so abruptly she almost fell. Once she was steady on her feet, she walked slowly down the hall and down the stairs into the master bedroom.

Wishing she'd handled things differently, she sat on the floor and brought her knees to her chest. Rocking back and forth, she felt tears splash down her cheeks. Why was she crying? She didn't even know these people.

Twice, Connor came and knocked.

Twice, she told him to go away.

He returned an hour later. "They're gone. They were very understanding. You were great. I'll be upstairs in my office—working," he said. "If you need me, you know where to find me. I'll take care of Taylor until you feel better."

"Thank you," she whispered, grateful to him for that, at least.

Ten

It was nearly four before Anna rose, washed her face, combed her hair and opened the door. After checking on Taylor, who thankfully was asleep, she stole upstairs and knocked softly on Connor's closed door.

"Connor?"

When he didn't answer, she lowered her hand and was about to rattle his doorknob when she heard deep, male voices from inside the room. Guerra and Connor were discussing a case involving insurance fraud.

"Okay, I say you step it up a notch. Rent the next-door house," Connor said. "Pretend you're his nosy new neighbor. Win his trust. Become his best friend...hell, use whatever pretext you have to. Meanwhile, keep your video handy, bag his trash and put a tail on him."

"What about privacy issues?"

"I think we'll be okay if we…"

She didn't want to hear more. She didn't like being reminded that deceit was part of Connor's profession and that he'd used such techniques to initiate their relationship.

She knocked louder, jiggling the doorknob, as well, before pushing it open. "I hope I'm not bothering you," she whispered.

Guerra strode toward her. "We're through, Mrs. Storm. I'm leaving."

With a curt nod, she smiled as he swept past her.

Connor, who was sitting at his desk, remained perfectly still, his handsome face guarded. "Better now?"

"I'm sorry."

"It's okay." His deep voice was gentle.

"I disappointed everybody."

"You've been through a lot. They understand. We rescheduled the meeting for next week. There will be a dinner party at the ranch. Abby helped me choose a caterer. In fact, I just got off the phone with them. It's all set up. You won't have to do a thing."

"Except show up," she whispered, feeling new dread as she remembered how shy she'd felt. No matter what Connor said, it was difficult to believe how they could possibly understand…when she herself was so confused.

His smile reflected her intensity. "They already love you," he said.

She swallowed tightly.

"Next week your father, Terence, will be able to come. Apparently, he's in Colombia interviewing trigger-happy terrorists in some jungle. If you ask me, ever since you were kidnapped, he's had something of a death wish. Abby thought he might take an interest in her baby son, Caesar, but apparently not even the little boy can draw him out of his shell. She says his heart was broken when he lost you."

Anna's chest felt tense and painful. It was as if she wanted to cry, and couldn't. "I…I don't know what to say. I can't imagine how seeing me now could possibly help him. I can offer him zero comfort. I…I don't know how to love people."

His expression was grim. "You love Taylor, don't you?"

"She's a baby. Babies are easy to love."

"Well, then you've got a good start in learning how to love. You're his little girl, just as Taylor's yours. Imagine if Taylor were kidnapped and you were in his shoes."

"No! Please—can we just talk about something else…anything besides my family?" She took a deep breath.

"Sure. Like what?"

"Like what? Oh, maybe like what have you been doing up here while I was downstairs?"

"Arranging the party for next week. Thinking about us. About where we go from here. I thought we should focus on solutions instead of problems, so I did a search on your old boyfriend, D. Crawford. You'll be happy to know he's moved on. He's got a wife and a job and a kid now. They live in Seattle. So, I guess you've got one less man on your tail."

Her throat tightened. "Thank you…for doing that, for telling me."

"I've been researching local teaching training programs. And U of H looks interesting. You might want to check it out."

When she saw that the University of Houston's Web page was open, she stiffened.

He shifted his long legs, crossing them. Then he leaned back and stared at the Web page instead of her, as if he were as uncomfortable in her presence as she was in his.

"I'm sorry for the way I manhandled you in the kitchen earlier. That move probably didn't put you in the best mood to meet your family." His low voice was gruff, his cheeks flushed. He didn't look up.

Studying his wide shoulders and the rigid tension in his ramrod posture, she wondered what he was really feeling.

"I'm no worse for wear, I guess," she said aloud.

The knuckles of his tanned hand clenching the mouse were bone-white. "I fed Taylor. I think she's down for a while."

"Thanks. You're good with her." She paused, not knowing what else to say. "I saw you put up her swing."

"Maybe we could let her try it out later."

"It was nice of you to go to so much trouble for her," she said.

"Nice?" he muttered, his tone suddenly a little harsh, his eyes flashing. "She's my daughter, too—a fact you seem anxious to forget."

"No. I—I'm not anxious to forget that. Not anymore. I didn't mean to insult you. I was trying to say thank-you."

In the awkward silence she listened to his computer hum, to the rush of cool air flowing from the vent above her head.

"So, why on earth would you trouble yourself to research teaching programs?" she asked.

He looked at her. "What are you going to do with the rest of your life? Run? Hide? Clean hotel rooms? Take care of old ladies? Live hand-to-mouth?"

"I—"

"You told me you wanted to be a teacher. That won't ever happen if you don't set goals and make plans."

"It was just a foolish dream."

"Not if we worked together to make it a reality." His deep voice sounded so easy and natural, as if he truly believed they could be a normal couple despite the way their marriage had begun; despite the fact that he held her here by force.

"Come over here and look at this," he said. "U of H also has online classes. You wouldn't even have to leave Taylor to go to the campus some semesters."

"School costs a lot of money. I have to work."

"I would be happy to support you while you went to school."

"But degrees take four years. That would mean—"

"A future together. Living as man and wife—"

"For four years?"

"Or longer. Would that be so awful?" His burning eyes held hers. "I would work very hard to give Taylor a secure, happy childhood."

Like the childhood when she'd had a twin sister whose hand she'd held while they'd skipped together?

Anna took a swift breath. "But why would you do that for me?"

"Because, as I keep telling you, I believe your dreams are important—not just to you, but to Taylor and to me. If you're not happy and fulfilled by doing something you love, you won't be a happy mother. And if you make the sacrifice to get your degree, you'll probably inspire Taylor to do the same in the future. I want that for her. That and much more. You need to be independent and confident instead of filled with insecurities that have to do with your past. Wouldn't you be more confident if you had a career you were proud of?"

His reasons were logical.

"I want Taylor to be proud of you. It's easy for her to love you now, but when she's older, trust me, you might be pretty glad you have a few accomplishments she can admire."

"I don't know."

"You have to charge ahead to get anywhere. The world is complicated," he said. "Job skills come in handy. If we remain married for now, you'd have your family and me. Taylor would have her father, who wants to be part of her life. You could have it all, Anna, if you'd let yourself."

Could she? What about love? He hadn't mentioned love. Her chest tightened until each breath hurt. Did she want his love?

Holding her hand to her mouth, she walked over to the window. Looking out at the street, she raised her fingertips to the windowpane. Behind her, she heard him shove his chair back.

"You don't have to be so alone anymore," he whispered. Striding across the room, he caught her by the shoulders and pulled her back against him.

Her heart sped up. She took another deep breath, but it did little to calm her. Her hips against his pelvis made her nerves jump.

"You're making this too hard. Why can't you let me fight some of your battles? Help make *impossible* dreams come true? Who knows, maybe we could even make each other happy someday."

Again she imagined them at the backyard swing with Taylor on summer evenings. She turned. His golden hair glistened in the slanting sunlight. She wanted nothing more than to slide her fingers through its thickness.

Her breath came unevenly. Her body trembled from the pressure of his hands on her arms, from the heat of his lean, muscular body.

"I can't forget you forced me to come here," she whispered, shoving him away.

His face hardened as he let her go. "You needed a push in the right direction. We have a daughter. I'll do anything to convince you that for your own good and for Taylor's, you've got to change."

"We were doing just fine before you showed up," she said, backing toward the door.

"Like hell." He pushed his hair back from his brow. "You're what Leo calls a hard dog."

One hand clasping the door, she turned and stared up into his smoldering eyes. "Hard dog?"

"Sorry. It's sort of a hunting term. Leo and I keep bird dogs to use when we hunt on the ranch. Leo trains the dogs with electrified collars. He gives them commands, and if they don't obey, he buzzes them."

"That's cruel."

When she took a step backward, he followed, cornering her with his body again, this time against the wall beside the door.

"But effective. Most dogs learn after one jolt. Some dogs, however, have to have several." His gaze swept her. "Leo calls them hard dogs."

"I'm not sure I like the comparison."

"Look, I can't even begin to imagine what you've been through, but I believe that we should try to make our marriage work for Taylor."

"For eighteen months I've distrusted everything about my attraction for you. It's hard to stop."

"Believe me, I thought I was a fool because of you, too. Why don't we both put all that in the past?"

He was standing too close, so close she felt like she was sinking in quicksand. What if she agreed?

What if she started to hope, to believe that he might always be there for her, no matter what?

"Why did you marry me, Anna?"

"I—I—"

"Why?"

As his gaze devoured her, a multitude of conflicting emotions tore her. Hope. Fear. Doubt. And something else that was bright and strong and fresh.

"Maybe you were trying to make that leap," he said.

For a long moment she felt mesmerized by his intense blue eyes.

"Too bad I found out you lied," she said.

"Ever think maybe that's not what really scared you? That you would have run even if I hadn't lied? I was getting too close, wasn't I?"

"No... No!"

"The kidnappers scared you so badly you blocked them out of your mind. You were a little girl when they took you. But you got away. You survived. And mere survival was enough for years and years. Until me. Until Taylor. Now you need more."

She remembered running in the woods, crying in the

dark, and nobody had come for her. At least not the people she'd loved and trusted, people whom she'd believed would be there for her forever.

"You don't know what it feels like to be weak and little and afraid...and so alone. You've always been strong, forceful."

"I lost my mother and my father young. I didn't have a friend in the world."

"You had Leo."

"I watched people die in Afghanistan. I was holding Linda, praying for her life when she died in my arms."

"But you were there for her. You were the hero in Afghanistan, kicking down doors. You saved lots of little children, I bet. Nobody came for me, do you understand? I wanted them to, but I got away all by myself!"

"They tried to find you."

"They failed."

"I found you, Anna. Maybe it's time you stopped being so afraid of loving."

His deep voice soothed her and seduced her on some primal level, but she fought those feelings. "You can't tell me what to do or how to feel! If I let myself believe in you again, if I let myself love you, and you walk out, what will I have left?"

"That's not going to happen."

"You don't know," she said. "Bad things can happen at any moment."

"Yes, they can! None of us has a guarantee. That's why we have to grab what's good. I think maybe if we tried, you and I might be good together, Anna. And that would be good for Taylor. Children thrive on love. I think you believe this, too, and that's what scares you. But if you won't try, we'll be doomed from the start."

"Then we're doomed," she said. "Because I don't want you or this marriage—as I've told you time and time again."

Eleven

Connor avoided Anna for the rest of the afternoon and evening. He ordered pizza, which he ate alone. Only after she heard him go back up to his office did Anna steal into the kitchen and eat a cold, leftover slice. Much later when he'd finally come to bed, and she'd met his eyes, his had been hard and cold. He hadn't smiled or kissed her or apologized or pulled her close, so she hadn't apologized, either.

Why should she apologize when this impossible marriage was all his fault? For hours she lay stiffly beside him, resenting him and yet hating that she'd made him so angry.

Then she fell asleep and dreamed about him. In her dream they were in his backyard, and he was pushing her in a swing. Garlands of flowers dripped from the trees, and every time she turned around to look at him, she smiled.

Happiness suffused her being, and her lips were curved

when she awakened beside him the next morning and felt
the heat of his body enveloping her. His back was to her.
For a lengthy moment, she stared longingly at his broad
shoulders. More than anything she wanted to touch his
skin, to feel his warmth.

Still, the last thing Anna expected was for him to roll
over, pull her close and kiss her as if he, too, had had
pleasant dreams, as if their quarrel had never happened.

Warm joy filled her.

"What do you say we call another truce and get the hell
out of here?" he said as he pressed his mouth to her temple.
"Take the baby…"

"But where would we go?" she asked, feeling unsure
and yet not wanting to fight with him anymore, either.

She got out of bed and pulled on her robe.

"Lunch. Car shopping. Phone shopping. You could use
some pretty new clothes. We could have dinner. We could
go anywhere. Everywhere."

She was about to protest when she remembered her
dream and caught herself. He was trying to be nice. And
she liked that. It would be wonderful to share a carefree
afternoon with him.

"Okay," she agreed softly, her heart filling with happiness.

Maybe Anna was tired of fighting. Maybe any girl who
was used to working menial jobs while rearing a baby
would enjoy a day spent eating out, buying clothes at the
Galleria and shopping car lots. Whatever the reason, the
day with Connor went surprisingly well.

Houston, with its spaghettilike freeways looping past
the impressive downtown and uptown skylines and posh

neighborhoods nestled amidst lush, tall pine trees, seemed like a young, energetic city. The sky was a deep blue. Connor said the air lacked its usual humidity and steamy quality. He commented on the traffic, saying it was lighter than usual.

"Maybe God is smiling on us," he said.

"You believe in—"

"I've witnessed more than my share of miracles. None to compare to Taylor, though. She proves that just being alive is a miracle."

To her surprise, she realized she agreed. And for a while, it almost seemed they were a normal couple.

While Connor drove them from lot to lot, she found her resentments had vanished and she talked to him with the same ease she had in Vegas, about the lonely years before she'd met him. For his part, he told her more about his own childhood, about growing up on the ranch he'd been thrown off of. He talked about his mother, who had died, and how he'd longed to have a family ever since. He confided more about Linda to her.

"When I buried them—Linda and our unborn baby—I never thought I'd get a second chance," he murmured, just as he stopped at another car lot. "I was bitter for a while and afraid of the future. But in the end I learned you can get over anything—if you want to bad enough."

"Maybe you can get past things," she murmured. "You're the big marine who kicks down doors. You think you can get what you want by force. It's not so easy for some of us."

"Different people have different kinds of courage. I think you're very brave."

She laughed.

"I'm serious." His blue eyes grew too intense for her to bear.

Suddenly she was in a hurry to choose a car, so she picked out the first car they looked at, a brand-new, blue Toyota sedan with a creamy, butter-soft leather interior. When the deal was closed and Connor dropped the keys into her palm, she was too shyly thrilled to know how to react.

"I don't know what to say," she whispered, not daring to meet his shining eyes as her hand slowly closed around the keys. "Thank you. I…I've never driven anything but a clunker before."

"Then you deserve a nice car." The way he said it, coupled with the way he looked at her, made her stomach flutter with unwanted excitement.

Then Taylor shrieked in a way that suggested, new car or not, she probably couldn't last much longer without a meal or a nap or the freedom to crawl.

"It's late. I think we'd better go home," Anna said, distrusting her softer feelings for him. "Before our little monster in her pink princess suit erupts."

Connor nodded, but clearly he didn't really get it, or maybe he didn't want to end their pleasant afternoon. So, when he saw a cell phone shop, he insisted on stopping. The wait and the long-winded salesman indeed proved too much for Taylor, who began to shriek and pull at her princess onesie.

Connor grabbed the first phone the man had shown him and said he'd buy it. On their way home, they chose a fast-food place, which Anna suggested solely because it had a playscape where Taylor could suck on a bottle and watch the big kids race and climb. Anna had a fruit parfait, and he ate a cheeseburger, and they talked even more. Why was it so much fun just doing ordinary things with him?

When they came home at last, they fed Taylor again and put her to bed. Then deftly negotiating the dark corridors and floating stairs, Connor led Anna into his living room where he put on music and pulled her into his arms.

Meeting her family here in this room was forgotten. In a trancelike state Anna clung to him as he spun her around beneath the tall ceilings and before the huge glass windows that let in the moonlight. Inevitably, dancing, their bodies glued to one another in that sparkling room, led to lovemaking.

As always when he held her and kissed her, she felt a secret, breathless joy that made her forget how he'd deliberately deceived her and then forced her to come here. As always his touch and the passion he aroused made her ache for more.

Afterward, when they were both spent, he pulled her close and held her tightly.

"I wish we could always be like we've been today," he said. "I had fun."

So had she. Being with him had seemed so easy. She'd felt young and happy. But what had any of it meant?

When she kissed his cheek lightly but said nothing, he let her go.

Slowly, his breathing became more regular, and he, who knew exactly what he wanted and demanded it, drifted to sleep, while she stared at the ceiling for hours, wondering what to do.

Could she let herself trust in him or in her foolish daydreams? What did they really have together? Were two weeks in Vegas based on lies, a daughter and his determination to force her to live with him enough to build a marriage on?

Maybe.

Maybe not. Or maybe she needed another option, like a job that was as far away as possible from Houston, Texas.

The idea possessed her to such an extent that thirty minutes later she stole out of bed. Pulling on her robe, she tiptoed upstairs to his office, booted his computer and began to search for employment possibilities.

It was way past time for her to take control of her life again.

Twenty-four hours later

Anna checked her watch. It was eight o'clock. Taylor was asleep. After devoting himself to his daughter and wife all day, Connor was now upstairs in his office, playing catch-up with his mail.

Dark shadows lurked in every corner of the garage as Anna crept into her car. Inhaling the new-car smell, she punched in a number on her new cell phone.

Instead of a person, she got a man's voice mail.

"I saw your ad for a caregiver, and I may need a job in the near future," Anna whispered. "I e-mailed you my résumé today." She left her name and her cell phone number and said she might be able to start in a few weeks. "I have a baby. I'm not sure if I will be bringing her or not. She might be staying with her father, at least for a while."

She stopped, startled, her heart skipping a beat. Leave Taylor? With him? Even for a little while? Where had that thought come from?

But why not leave Taylor with Connor if they separated and needed to adjust to the idea of divorce? He longed to get to know Taylor better. He was good with her. For the past two days, daughter and father had flirted constantly. No longer did Anna fear Connor deepening his bond with his child.

After Anna hung up, she went into the nursery and hovered over Taylor, who looked like a little angel as she clutched her blanket while she slept in the moonlight. She would have to start weaning Taylor immediately.

The man called back while Anna stood staring down at her precious child.

He described the job, which was a menial caregiver position in faraway Georgia. An old man who was dying needed a sitter. The job didn't pay much, but the granddaughters thought a baby would cheer their grandfather no end.

So, she could bring Taylor.

Or not.

Anna told him she'd have to let him know in a few days.

Twelve

Little Spur Ranch
Near Bastrop, Texas

Seven days had flown by. A horde of caterers had come and gone earlier in the day. Now the house was redolent with the scent of cooked roast and herbs and spices, even all the way back here in the master bedroom, where Anna sat before her mirror, holding a pair of earrings.

The dining-room table was set. Their dinner, covered in foil, needed only to be heated up.

Tonight at 7:00 p.m., Abby, Leo and Terence would arrive and knock on their front door.

Her hand trembling a little, Anna leaned forward to attach one of the white loop earrings that matched her sundress. All week she'd tried to prepare for tonight, but her chest was tight, her stomach uneasy. Last night a woman, a Mrs. Drake, had called, frantically begging Connor for his help because her husband had been kidnapped. Not that Anna, who was sympathetic, was concentrating on the woman's plight.

"Boo, baby girl!"

Connor's deep, tender voice and Taylor's flirtatious squeals of joy drifted in through the partially open windows. Connor had been the completely devoted father and husband all week. This afternoon he'd spread a large blue quilt on the shady front lawn for the baby so Anna could have the ranch house to herself to get her head together. Even now he was dutifully playing peep-eye.

Did all fathers spend so much time playing with their daughters? Or researching toys and books for them?

He'd bought several books about childhood development, and he'd actually read them. Damn the man. Was he trying to make it impossible for her to walk out on him?

Determined to finish dressing, she leaned toward her mirror again to secure the second hoop earring. Just when she thought she had it, it slipped through her fingers.

Sinking down onto the stool of her dressing table, Anna tried to calm herself, but at every joyous giggle from her daughter, at every teasing comment from Connor, she started.

Although they hadn't fought about her wanting to divorce him again, she imagined the idea was never far from Connor's mind, as it wasn't from hers.

Maybe she would have tried to reopen the discussion last night, but the news of Larry Drake's kidnapping had knocked her for a loop.

When she'd walked outside after supper and had stared up at the moon, Connor had followed her. Then she'd turned and seen him there, so tall and handsome, his presence so reassuring she'd flown into his arms and clung, her hands shaking a little.

"Pretty night," he'd said, holding her close.

"Yes," she'd agreed, nestling against him, treasuring the safety of his hard, warm body. She wanted to stay there forever.

"Shouldn't you postpone our little dinner and help that poor woman find her husband?"

"I have my best men assigned to the Drake case. Nothing is more important to me than you and Taylor and your family. Not to mention Leo and Abby. We all need to get this dinner behind us."

Anna loved his ranch, and in spite of her best intentions not to enjoy herself around her husband, she'd loved every minute she'd spent with him this past week.

He'd been so attentive and sweet to her and to Taylor. Proudly, he'd walked them over every inch of the property, pointing out new fences, barns and freshly cut pastures. They'd taken turns pushing Taylor in her stroller or carrying her when Taylor stretched her arms toward them to be picked up.

Even when he'd had to work, she'd been happily conscious of his presence in a nearby room or outside. Most mornings when he'd connected with his office, she'd bathed and fed Taylor and tidied the kitchen.

How she'd looked forward to the afternoons because that was the time he'd devoted himself wholly to Taylor and her.

Instead of using forceful tactics, he'd been deliberately

wooing her. She should have stopped him, she knew; fought with him. But she couldn't.

The nights had been the most wonderful part. After they'd put Taylor down, the intimate candlelit dinners they'd shared on the terrace or in the dining room had led to lovemaking.

Even the nights Taylor had refused to go to bed early had been fun. They'd played with her until all three of them had collapsed together in the master bedroom. After Taylor had finally fallen asleep, Connor had carried her to her own bed and returned to make love to Anna.

He'd bought both of them lots of presents, which had meant more to Anna than they would have if she'd had family who'd remembered birthdays and Christmas. When Anna told him she didn't need so many clothes, he'd said, "You're a beautiful woman, why shouldn't you have beautiful clothes? I have plenty of money, and I want to show you off. So, don't worry about it."

But if she wasn't going to stay in this marriage, how could she have accepted all his gifts, each one touching her heart too much after a lifetime of no presents?

Every time she thought about leaving him, a tight lump formed in her throat. To distract herself, Anna got up and twirled to examine the back of the strapless sundress Connor had bought for her in Austin last week and suggested she wear tonight.

"Why this dress?" she'd asked him earlier when he'd pulled it out of the closet.

He'd held it against her body. "Because you look so damn sexy in it." The heat in his eyes and hands when he'd shaped the soft fabric against her breasts had made her skin flame.

He'd let the sundress fall to the Saltillo tile floor. Then he'd cupped her buttocks and pulled her against him so she could feel his arousal. "Taylor's napping, right?" His eyes gleaming with that possessive look that was so thoroughly disturbing, he'd slid his Stetson back on his forehead and had hugged her closer.

"She seemed pretty tired when I put her down."

He'd chuckled. "Sounds like a window of opportunity."

Her blood singing, Anna had thrown back her head and made her mouth available. When his tongue slid inside to mate with hers, she'd had to have him right then.

He'd begun to kiss her as he unbuttoned her blouse, his mouth moving from her lips, to her neck, to her nipples, which had peaked when he'd twirled his wet tongue across them. Soon she'd been naked in his arms, lost to the world, conscious only of his warm hands, hot looks and expert caresses during those gentle hours of the early afternoon.

"How about the kitchen table?" he'd whispered. "Since you caused that fantasy, you owe me," he'd teased.

She'd known she should have said no, but she'd laughed and said, "We'd better make sure all the caterers are gone. Wouldn't want to shock anybody."

He'd chuckled. Then he'd kissed her.

After making excellent use of the sturdy table, he'd carried her to bed where she'd lain cuddled up against him, her head resting in the curve of his broad shoulder. Just remembering how his body had felt made her want to fast-forward into climbing into bed with him again tonight.

Seven o'clock. Think about that, not sex with a husband you might leave, you lovesick fool.

Tonight their dinner guests included Leo, Abby and their toddler son, Caesar, as well as Terence, who'd flown in from South America.

"Abby picked your father up last night," Connor had said over breakfast.

Abby, he'd explained, owned a branding firm in Austin, and Leo spent most of his time at the corporate offices of the Golden Spurs in San Antonio. They'd spend the night along with Terence at the Buckaroo Ranch. This ranch had belonged to Abby before their marriage and was right next door to the Little Spur.

Suddenly Anna was tired of thinking about her family. She needed to get outside and try to relax a little before they came.

The sound of pots banging and Connor's teasing tone floated inside.

"Boo!"

When Taylor squealed, Anna rushed to the window. Taylor was lying on her back, her chubby legs kicking at Connor as he leaned over her on that sun-dappled quilt. Her tiny hand closed around his finger and held on tight. They looked so happy as they stared at each other that she wanted to run outside and sink down beside Connor and revel in their love for each other.

Anna took a deep breath. Suddenly she saw a little girl with a bouncy ponytail and a pink backpack holding tightly to Connor's big tanned hand as he proudly walked her up to a big brick elementary school. With all her heart Anna wanted to be holding Taylor's other hand on that all-important day.

If Anna stayed with Connor and they became a real family, there would be a lifetime of shared holidays and milestones to treasure. They might have more children, maybe a little boy with blue eyes and a dimple.

Anna's fingers curled tightly against the windowpane. Then she jerked her hand away and rushed down the hall to the front door.

She felt an urgent need to get outside so she could be with Taylor and Connor—now.

Thirteen

The screen door banging behind her, Anna ran out onto the wide gallery that wrapped the large, white, Spanish-style ranch house. The sun was too high and hot, and she'd forgotten her sunglasses. Putting her hand to her brow to shield her eyes, she searched the lawn for Connor.

Despite the white glare, she saw that except for Connor's Stetson and Taylor's toys and pots and pans, the blue quilt was empty. When Connor and Taylor didn't seem to be inside the tall white walls that surrounded the house, she called Connor's name. A board creaked at the far end of the porch behind her.

"Over here," Connor drawled.

"I didn't see you."

"Well, now you do," he said lazily. "I was just reading Taylor a book."

Dressed in a snug, white T-shirt that molded his muscular torso and jeans, he was rocking Taylor in the shade on the big porch swing while he held a board book open. Even though her little hands were fisted and raised in an effort to fight naptime, Taylor's heavy lids hovered at half-mast.

Anna smiled back at him. "So, you wore her out," she said, trying to make her voice sound normal and light.

"At least she's happy. How are you doing?" he asked.

"Oh! I'm fine," she said. "I just need some air. I—I thought maybe I'd see how you two were doing and then maybe go for a walk…before…they…our guests…arrive. Compose myself."

"It's awfully hot if you're not in the shade."

"I won't melt."

"I like the way you melt." The smoldering blue light in his eyes made her think of their nights together when she lay underneath him; made her want more nights in the future.

She licked her dry lips.

"Sorry we can't take another nap," he said, his low voice charged. "Don't go too far. You look too pretty in that sundress to be out in this heat."

"Thank you for taking care of Taylor so I could get ready. She does love the way you tease and flirt with her."

"No more than I love her big smiles. She's a natural-born Southern Belle, if ever there was one. Notwithstanding her great talent as a drummer." His blue eyes softened as he looked from her to their child. "I'm already dreading all the boyfriends she'll have when she grows up."

At the thought of their uncertain future, Anna's stomach tightened. "Well…"

"Have a good walk."

Feeling reluctant to leave them, Anna headed down the stairs anyway. Part of her wanted to offer to make a pitcher of lemonade and then sink down on that swing beside them.

She straightened her shoulders and headed down the path toward the gate.

At the end of the gravel path, she opened the gate. Keeping to the narrow road that wound beneath the thick, spreading branches of the live oaks, she left the white house behind.

When she saw a bench under a live oak tree near the fence line where several fat Santa Cruz cattle were grazing, she sat down in the shade.

A breeze swept across the pasture, and she relaxed, contentment filling her as she watched the cattle munch grass. She drew her knees up. Hugging her legs against her chest, she soon lost track of time.

Suddenly the earth thundered, startling her out of her reverie. She jumped up from the bench just as a slim, young woman, her dark blond hair flying behind her as she rode a palomino bareback, galloped out of the trees.

Abby.

Breathless, Anna got up and stepped closer to the fence.

Abby's slim hand tugged on the reins. When she was no more than ten feet away from the fence, the palomino stopped and pawed the earth.

Abby dismounted wordlessly. Leading the palomino by the long reins, she headed toward the fence, too.

Anna wanted to run toward her twin and yet away from her at the same time. Her mouth curved shyly.

"Becky? Are you feeling better? I'm so looking forward to our dinner."

We're like strangers. We shouldn't be strangers. We should have shared our lives.

The palomino snorted.

Waves of feelings and images rushed at Anna. She saw two little girls, their dark blond braids bouncing on their thin shoulders, as they rode Abby's horse bareback along hot, dusty streets in the middle of summer. She remembered them standing side by side on the edge of a swimming pool, both of them holding their noses before they jumped in at the same time. She remembered them helping their mother bake cookies for Santa Claus.

The girls carrying a tray of cookies for Santa to the Christmas tree dissolved. Suddenly Anna was standing under a live oak staring at the strange yet familiar face of her adult twin.

There was so much she wanted to tell her twin, Anna felt like she was about to burst. And yet…and yet…

"Abby?"

Air rushed into Anna's throat, swelled, pushed, but she couldn't get it out.

So many years lost. Too many. They'd been so close once, sharing everything. Nothing could make up for what they'd lost. It was as if she'd locked up all the love she'd felt for Abby and had thrown away the key.

Loneliness washed over Anna. The sadness from not knowing her twin overwhelmed her, and yet Abby was here now. Abby seemed to want a relationship with her.

Maybe the least she could do was try to find some common ground with her twin.

"Are you feeling better?" Abby asked.

Anna nodded. "Being here at the ranch has been great. Peaceful."

"We love it here. It'll be nice when Caesar and Taylor are older and can run about freely exploring, the way we used to. Kids hate all the constraints of life in the city."

Anna smiled. "I guess I'd better check on reheating our dinner."

"Sure. See you," Abby whispered. "Come over anytime."

Anytime? Was such a relationship possible? Could they just start where they were now? The idea was exciting. Well, why couldn't they?

Anna turned and ran lightly back to the sheltering, red-roofed house.

When she ran through the gate, Connor, who'd been on his cell phone, leapt from the swing.

"I'll call you back." Slamming his phone shut, he raced toward her.

"Sweetheart—"

She swerved and would have run past him if he hadn't stepped in front of the door.

"You okay?" he asked.

"I'm…fine."

Pulling her into his hard, warm arms, he pressed her face against his chest. "Did something happen?"

"I just saw Abby! She was riding her horse. Suddenly I remembered our childhood. We used to swim together, ride horses… The memories were fresh as yesterday. We were crazy about each other back then. Then she was all grown-up again, and I realized I don't even know her. I felt so much happiness. Then it hurt so much."

"This is a step. Dinner will be another step."

"I…I wish we could put dinner off."

"Which is exactly why we need to do it now. You're building it up in your mind too much."

"It feels forced. Just like our marriage feels forced."

"Does it? Do you really mean that? Or are you just saying that to protect yourself? Because every time I touch you or we make love, it's too perfect for words. Why do you think that is?"

"I don't know. I don't care."

"Well, damn it, I do! What we have is special. You need to face your family whether you're ready to or not. The next time you see them, it will be easier."

"I can't."

"I could tell you awful stories about *can't*. It's always fatal to think *can't*. I've seen people die because of it."

He pressed Anna's hand to his lips. "I'll be right beside you." Wrapping her in his arms, he held her for a long moment until she began to cling.

"Everything can be taken away in a heartbeat," she whispered. "I can't risk myself to that again."

"Don't think like that. Why not think that maybe you and I have had our share of bad luck? That maybe we're due? That loving…living…is a risk worth taking? That you and Taylor and me could be your second chance?"

Could they?

"Just hold me," she whispered. "Just hold me."

"Anna, I'm sorry I lied to you in Vegas. It's my fault as much as yours we got off to a bad start."

She thought about the job possibility in Georgia. Then he began stroking her hair and kissing her brow, and she clung to him even tighter.

Fourteen

Connor tensed as he watched Terence and Abby crowd Anna. At least she was in the room this time. Still, he didn't like the way her eyes burned too brightly in her thin, ethereal face and darted toward the door.

Don't push. Give her room, space.

Connor hoped that the dinner tonight would go well. So much was at stake.

He wanted one thing—to wake up every morning for the rest of his life with Anna's soft, warm body wrapped in his, with his daughter in her room down the hall. But no matter how hard he'd tried these past few days to win Anna over, he still didn't feel sure of her.

If only she'd connect to her family tonight. Maybe then she'd decide to look to the future.

Much as Connor wanted the evening to succeed, no

sooner had Connor opened the door than Terence and Abby had pounced on Anna, who now stood mute as a mesquite stump as she clutched Taylor too tightly. Then Caesar toddled into the great room inspecting things, and Leo chased after him, standing guard.

"I love your dress," Abby was saying too animatedly to Anna.

"Yeah, you look great," Terence, Anna's father, agreed, looking anywhere but at Anna.

"We couldn't believe it when we heard Connor had found you. And Taylor," Abby said. "She's so beautiful, by the way."

When Abby fingered the hem of Taylor's smocked dress, Taylor closed her eyes and shyly buried her face against her mother's neck.

"Sometimes she does this with strangers when she's tired," Anna said, glancing at Connor again. "She thinks if she shuts her eyes, they'll vanish."

"We're not strangers, little darling," Abby said. "We met you last week. I'm your aunt Abby."

"How about drinks?" Connor said, hoping liquor would ease some of the tension.

When nobody replied, he seized Anna by the elbow. Ushering her into the great room where Leo had already disappeared along with Caesar, the others had no choice but to follow.

Big mistake. Maybe the room with its large, masculine, leather couches and its overbearing antler chandelier was perfect for large gatherings, but it was horrible for this tense little crowd. Long shadows looming against the walls and the vast spaces made it too easy for Anna and Terence to hide.

"Ladies, what will you have?" Connor asked cheerily.

"Water," Anna mumbled, not looking at him.

"Me, too," Abby said.

"With ice," Anna whispered in a lost, quiet voice.

"Yes, lots of ice," Abby agreed with false gaiety.

As if anybody in their frozen group needed ice.

Help me here, people! Connor thought.

Anna took her drink and curled up at one end of an oversize couch. Taking the hint, Abby sat at the other end. Anna set her drink down and then let Taylor wiggle to the ground. Catching Anna's uneasy mood, Abby's mouth tightened. Then she forced a smile and stared down at her niece.

"She's so cute," Abby said. "How many teeth?"

"One." Anna looked away. "Maybe two, soon." Abby couldn't seem to think of anything else to say, so the two sisters just sat there, unsure of each other.

It was going to take a lot of love and patience and time to sort it all out.

The sun must have come out from behind a cloud because suddenly a bright, amber beam slashed downward from the high windows above the staircase and lit up Connor's prized miniature Steuben Longhorn.

Caesar's eyes brightened. With a joyous yelp, Leo's black-haired replica waddled toward the sparkling crystal cow on the coffee table.

Did all kids run before they could walk? Or was his nephew the only one who was hell on wheels? Would Taylor take after him? Connor wanted them to know each other, to play together.

"No, young man! That is not a toy!" Smiling at Anna

before dashing to the rescue, Abby snatched the little cow a nanosecond before Caesar's small, chubby fingers could touch it.

"No!" she repeated in a sterner tone, handing the cow to Anna.

Caesar's mouth drooped. He was prone to fits when crossed. With a low growl, he threw himself on the floor.

Connor fought to suppress a smile. "Does he take after his stubborn father, or what?"

"Or maybe his uncle," Leo said.

Caesar growled again.

"No, sir! Young man, you are not to make that sound to your mother!" Abby chided.

Caesar's bottom lip protruded at a dangerous angle. Fortunately, Taylor shrieked and clapped with such admiration at his antics that his need for a tantrum diminished.

Pleased to find himself with an ardent fan, he beamed. Standing up, he ran over to her. Mimicking his mother, he shouted, "No!"

Taylor, who was warming up even if her mother wasn't, smiled and clapped.

"Careful. Your cousin's little," Leo said as he took Caesar's hand and led him away.

"Tawor," Caesar said, pulling his hand loose from his father's and clapping.

Caesar was into patty-cake big-time. Chortling, Taylor began to clap, too. Grinning from ear to ear, Caesar strutted up to each adult, and soon he had everybody clapping and saying patty-cake.

Thank God for babies! It was impossible to ignore the little clowns.

"It won't be long before you two will have to childproof the house," Abby said.

Connor nodded. "I hope so."

Anna frowned and refused to meet his eyes.

"Hey, did you notice I got the new fence up along the north pasture?" Leo asked.

The sudden vibration in his pocket again made Connor tense. Even though he ignored it, he knew he'd better return the call as soon as he could.

"I asked you what you thought about the new fence," Leo repeated.

"Sorry…er…thanks. How much do I owe you?" Connor asked.

"Our neighbor paid half, so a fourth. I'll e-mail you about it."

"Great," Connor said.

Why couldn't Anna say something? Why did she just sit there huddled at her end of his big couch?

Hey, she hasn't run. This is progress.

Still, her hands were playing with the folds in her skirt until she looked up and saw him watching her. Glancing down, she knotted her fingers in her lap.

Connor stood. "Can I get anybody another drink before dinner?"

Their ice cubes clinking, Terence and Leo held up their glasses. Connor slugged the last of his drink.

Great. The women were ignoring their water while the men slammed down Scotch.

Connor opened his cell phone and saw Guerra had called him, so he returned the call. When he hung up, Leo, who'd been listening, asked him about the Drake kidnapping. "So, where do you think he is?"

"We don't have many leads."

"His family must be going crazy…like we did," Terence said. "I remember how it eats away at you. You feel so helpless. You blame yourself. No matter where you are, you never forget."

A glass shattered on the Saltillo floor. "Sorry, Connor," Anna whispered.

"It's okay," he said, rushing to her side. "Are you okay?"

"Memories," she whispered. "They keep coming. Ever since I saw Abby today."

"Leo, watch Caesar while I get the glass up," Abby said.

"You want to know what happened to me…."

At Anna's hushed tone, everybody froze.

"Well, I don't know because I don't remember much. A white van…being scared…wanting to get away and hide. Feeling lost and forgotten…like I didn't matter anymore."

"Dear God!" Terence thundered.

"It's over. You're safe with us now," Abby said.

Terence set his drink down and walked over to Anna.

"You matter, Becky. You matter. I think I've been hiding, too," Terence said. "Maybe now that I know you're alive, I can stop."

Connor took a step backward so father and daughter could be together.

Slowly, Terence's arms came around Anna. She didn't put her arms around her father, but it was enough. Terence's movements were shy and awkward as he began patting her hair.

"You smell the same," Anna murmured in a shy, lost voice. "At least, something's the same."

"Cigarettes," he muttered. "Sorry about that. Hardest habit in the world to break."

"I remember you because of their smell. Don't ever quit."

"I won't tell my doctor you said that."

"Daddy!" Abby protested, but with a new light, teasing note in her voice. "You did promise me *and* your doctor you'd try to quit again."

Anna actually smiled.

"Two daughters, each telling me something different. Some things never change. Do you remember how you used to bicker about everything?"

Anna smiled, as if she were remembering happier times when her only problem had been competing with her twin to win their parents' affection.

"If I got a B on a paper and Abby got a B+, I'd tattle on her and tell you about something else she'd done wrong."

"Then she'd tell one on you."

Abby laughed.

Suddenly Anna looked tired from the effort of socializing.

"Excuse me," she said before she retreated down the hall.

Wanting to make sure she was all right, Connor caught up to her in the master bedroom. "How's it going?"

"It's hard...remembering how it was with my family and yet feeling like I barely know them."

"You're doing great."

"Am I? Or are you just saying that because you want to believe it?"

He caught her chin, lifting her head so she'd have to meet his eyes. "I'm trying to show you that you could have a life here with them. With me. They love you. And Taylor. I care about you, too."

"Do you? Don't you ever feel as trapped as I do? Don't you?"

When his expression darkened and he turned on his heel to rejoin the others, she regretted her harsh words. But it was too late to take them back.

For the rest of the evening he was polite to her in front of the others. But as the hour grew later and his eyes never sought hers, when she sensed he was deliberately distancing himself from her, she began to wish she'd handled things differently.

She hated making him miserable. What was she going to do to make things better?

Fifteen

The evening felt interminable. Anna's head was pounding as she stood beside Connor at their front door. Why couldn't her father just leave like everybody else?

"Goodbye," she whispered, pushing the door wider in the hope that Terence would finally take the hint.

But he just stood there, his heart in his troubled gaze as he studied her.

"I'm sorry. I really do have a headache," she said. Unable to think about his needs or Connor's a second longer, Anna raced off to the master bedroom, leaving Connor to see Terence out and lock up. She hated being rude or cruel, but she felt sick from strain.

"Dinner went better than I expected," Connor said when he joined her a few minutes later. "Things were a little tense at first, but…"

Blindly, she nodded as she swallowed an aspirin with water. "I really don't want to talk about it." Turning her back on him, she sat down at her dressing table and began to struggle with the clasp of her necklace.

When her hands began to shake, he walked up behind her. "Need some help?"

She didn't want his thoughtfulness, and when his warm fingers settled possessively at her nape, she fought the warm quickening of her pulse. In no time he had the necklace undone and was placing it on the countertop.

"You're awfully quiet," he said.

"Am I? Sorry!" All night she'd felt like she was being pulled in two. By them. By him. By their expectations. "Can we please just not talk anymore? About any of it?"

He nodded.

What she wanted was to get into bed, pull up the sheets and be still and quiet. Not that Leo and Abby and Terence weren't nice, because they were. And she'd felt intensely drawn to them. But they expected her to be their sister and daughter, and she still didn't know if she ever could be.

Maybe it was too late for them ever to be a family again. Maybe if she went away, they'd all be happier in the end—including Connor.

What she wanted now was the nothingness that a dreamless sleep could bring. Maybe in the morning she would know what to do.

When Connor quickly kissed her temple, his lips were too warm. They aroused too many unwanted longings.

She jerked free of his embrace. "I said I have a headache."

"Right." His blue eyes darkened. "I'm sorry to hear

that," he said, his tone harsher. "Maybe I'll leave you for a while then. I need to make some calls."

"Your kidnapping case?" She shuddered.

He nodded. "I imagine I'll be a while. You'll be all right?"

"I'll be fine," she lied.

"When I finish my calls, do you want me to stay in the guest bedroom? That way I won't wake you up when I come to bed."

Instantly, she felt hurt, almost rejected at his offer to sleep alone, which was crazy because he was giving her what she'd thought she wanted a second ago—space.

Fool. What she really wanted was him beside her, all night, his arms around her—because who knew how long they had?

"You're always so thoughtful," she said.

"I know you're tired, so I'll check on Taylor for you before I get on the phone."

"Sweet," she whispered, struggling to hide her desperation.

He smiled, flashing that beautiful smile. Straight white teeth. Virile masculinity. Tinged with white-hot, all-consuming desire for her. As always the vital, male emotion behind his smile heightened her conflicting feelings for him.

He wanted her, and she'd told him she preferred to sleep alone. When he turned to go, the fierce need that welled up inside her as he swaggered down the hall almost made her call him back.

"Don't go," she whispered, but too softly for him to hear. He'd been so nice, supporting her, planning everything, executing his plan perfectly. He'd stayed at her side all evening, playing their perfect host, smoothing things over even after their quarrel in the bedroom. He'd even promised to help her finish cleaning up in the kitchen tomorrow.

Her heart twisted.

In the morning, maybe she'd feel strong enough to figure out what she had to do.

Flashes of light in between bouts of suffocating darkness lit up the man's horrible, scarred face. His thin lips were cruel. His narrow, curved nose was more like a beak than any human's nose. And his eyes, which stared straight through her, shone with an unnatural, reddish light, and seemed dead at the center.

"Naughty girl!" he growled. "You took off your blindfold! You know what that means—you've seen me. Now I can never let you go!"

She woke up alone—screaming, the sound muffled by her pillow. More bad memories hit her.

Headlights on the wrong side of the road. A jarring crash. The van on its side.

She remembered crawling out of it and running. A truck had stopped. In the confusion, she'd climbed into the bed and had covered herself with a tarp. When the engine started she'd fallen asleep. When the truck had stopped hours later, she'd climbed out and had run into the woods. Her next memory was of being held in Sister Kate's arms.

I remember, she thought.

In a flash, Anna was out of bed, her bare feet running down the hall to the guest bedroom where she hoped Connor lay asleep. She was on the verge of pushing his door open and rushing to him, when she stopped herself.

Connor had forced her to resume their relationship. She couldn't keep running to Connor expecting him to save her, and then pushing him away. She had to decide what she wanted to do with the rest of her life, and maybe she would only be able to do that on her own. Maybe it would be best if she left him for a while. Maybe she should leave Taylor, too.

She walked slowly down to the nursery. Taylor was curled up, asleep beside her bottle. Anna lifted the bottle out of the crib. Taylor, who still wasn't used to the idea of bottles, hadn't drunk all of it.

Quietly Anna sang her the ABCs. Then soundlessly she patted her hands together and whispered patty-cake.

Suddenly tears at the thought of even a temporary separation filled Anna's eyes. She had to step back so they wouldn't splash onto Taylor's downy blond hair.

"I love you," she whispered. "You know that, don't you? If Mommy goes away for a little while, she loves you."

But what would Taylor think when she wasn't here tomorrow?

Tomorrow? No. She couldn't wait until the morning.

It took all of Anna's courage to square her shoulders and walk out of the nursery. Ten minutes later, carrying a single bag and her purse, she moved silently back down the hall past the guest room where Connor slept. She paused for a long moment. Then with a leaden heart, she tiptoed toward the kitchen and slipped quietly out of the back door.

I don't want to hurt you or my family, but I can't stay here right now. I need time to myself to think.

Maybe I want a divorce. One way or the other, I'll
call you in a few weeks so we can sort out what to
do about Taylor.
Anna

Cursing silently, Connor tore the note into pieces.

He picked up the phone and dialed Abby, because he
couldn't think of anybody else he could trust with Taylor
while he dealt with the Drake situation.

Don't think about Anna.

"One more step. Just one more," Connor mumbled en-
couragingly, as he and two of his men dragged a shivering
Larry Drake out of the last tight hole in the cave. Although
not as icy as Michael's Well, which was located in the lower
chamber of the cave, this larger, limestone chamber still felt
cold. Maybe that was because Connor and Drake were both
dripping wet from having been in the well too long.

Connor's teeth chattered. It had taken him two hours to
descend into the tight, slippery hell and climb back out.
Drake, who was probably in a state of shock, was so weak
he could barely stumble forward.

"Almost there!" Connor said. Then they staggered out
of the cave's opening.

A series of kaleidoscope flashes and sounds blinded and
deafened him. After the total blackness of Drake's watery
grave, the hill country sunlight was glorious dazzle. The
exhilarated crowd at the top raised beer cans, cheering.

A woman screamed joyously. "Larry!"

Connor took a deep breath of the sweet, juniper-scented
air. Ever since Anna's departure he'd been racing against

time to find Drake. Now that the ordeal was nearly over, Connor suddenly felt on the edge of collapse.

He wanted to go home to Anna, to hold her close, but she wasn't there.

Leigh Drake hurled herself at Connor. Cupping his face in her hands, she kissed him on both cheeks. "Thank you!"

Sobbing, she launched herself at her husband, who toppled to the ground in her arms. When she realized how weak he was, her tears rained harder, and she clung even tighter.

When cameramen rushed forward, Connor stepped in front of them, protecting the Drakes. "Give them a break, why don't you?"

For a minute longer Connor watched them hug and kiss again, wishing he had a wife who wanted him half that much. Then a reporter grabbed his arm and shoved a microphone in his face.

"How'd you know it was Jefferson, the watchman who got fired for drinking on the job?"

"We got lucky."

His men had interviewed dozens of employees. Guerra had talked to Mrs. Jefferson, since Jefferson couldn't be located. She'd nervously told Craig about Jefferson's fondness for spelunking and diving in Michael's Well.

Connor had played a long shot.

"How'd you figure out Drake was handcuffed at the bottom of Michael's Well?"

Bubbles.

"Finding Drake was nothing short of a miracle," Connor said. "He had two minutes of air left."

Connor turned away, ending the interview. He snapped his phone open to call Anna before it hit him again—hard.

She was gone.

Maybe she was divorcing him. Maybe not.

God hadn't given him a miracle where she was concerned.

Sixteen

Three days later
Houston, Texas

Twisting her head, Taylor was fighting the nipple of the bottle as Connor rocked her in the pink nursery, which now brimmed with stuffed bears and all sorts of neon-colored, battery-operated toys. The talking toys had loud voices and sang all sorts of cheerily obnoxious songs like the ABCs and "Twinkle, Twinkle, Little Star." Connor knew he'd bought way too many toys, but he wanted to console Taylor.

Connor wiggled the bottle. "I know it's not Mommy, but hey, it's food, honey," he pleaded wearily.

He wasn't as patient as Anna, and he felt sorry for Taylor. He didn't blame her for being furious at him because Anna had left them. Hell, maybe it *was* his fault.

Taylor's defiant blue eyes glared up at him as if she were begging him to solve their terrible problem. But when all he did was poke her bottom lip with that nasty nipple, causing a drop of the awful formula to pearl there, her brows shot together angrily and she mashed her face into his shoulder. When she finally came up for air, she took a sneak peek at him. Since Anna was nowhere in sight, Taylor fisted her hands and started kicking.

Soon, she began to kick harder and yell.

"Mamamamama…"

"I know, baby. She left me, too."

A lump formed in his throat as hopelessness warred with his bitter male pride. No matter how bad this got, no matter how sorry he felt for Taylor, he would not go after Anna.

How the hell could she have left their daughter, even for a little while?

Abby and Terence wanted him to search for her, but he wouldn't. Maybe it was her turn to call the shots. If she wanted out, he'd let her out.

He loved her. She wouldn't want to hear that, so he wouldn't tell her when she called, but he did.

She would stay in his heart forever. Even so, she lacked some essential strength he had to have in his mate—the grit to stick it out through thick and thin.

He dreaded her call. He hated the thought of hashing out custody arrangements and a divorce settlement, of dividing Taylor between them, but she wouldn't be the first child who had to deal with divorce.

As if Taylor read the stubborn set of his mind, she arched her back and began to kick at his chest and scream.

He set the bottle down on the floor beside the rocker and stood up. "Here we go again."

Lifting Taylor to his shoulder he began to pace. If anything, that just made Taylor madder. He picked up teddy bears, showed her colorful pictures on the wall, played her mobile, bounced a ball, made a toy duck squeak.

Taylor, who was not amused, yelled at him so loudly and turned so red and got so hot, he was afraid she might rupture something. Who knew that taking care of a small baby could be so terrifying?

He sighed in weary desperation. It looked like he was in for another hellish night. She'd been inconsolable the first two. Both nights she hadn't cried herself into a total state of exhaustion until around 3:00 a.m.

He stroked Taylor's fine, glossy curls, which he'd actually washed and dried all by himself two hours earlier without breaking her. Then he sat them back down and offered her the bottle again.

"Please eat. I don't want you to starve."

She fisted her hands and then batted the bottle so hard it fell and rolled across the floor. More tears spilled down her purple cheeks. Then Taylor began to make furious, truly frightening, strangling sounds.

"It's okay," he whispered. "It's okay."

But it wasn't, and maybe it wouldn't ever really be okay again.

"Why didn't anybody ever tell me that putting a diaper on a screaming kid is worse than branding a steer?" Connor said.

At least six ruined disposable diapers and torn pieces with tape lay in a wadded heap by the diaper pail.

"What we need here is a roll of duct tape," Leo teased. "And a lot more patience."

At the sound of her uncle's voice, Taylor cried even harder and kicked more furiously. Gently, Connor lifted her legs and slid the seventh diaper underneath her bottom.

"This isn't working, you know," Leo said in his CEO tone that brooked no argument. "You can't run your company and play superdaddy 24/7. You're way out of your league here."

"You're telling me."

"You've got to go after Anna."

The tape tore off the diaper. "Hell," Connor said. "I just wrote an ad for a nanny."

"Here! Give me that piece of tape! You're not supposed to tape the damn thing to her! No wonder she won't stop crying."

"She was wiggling."

"They always wiggle. Move! Let an expert take over!" Deftly Leo nudged his brother aside. Once he'd taped the diaper correctly, he stepped back, eyeing the diaper and then Connor triumphantly.

Connor opened the diaper pail and pitched the dirty one in it. Immediately a rank odor perfumed the pink nursery. Wrinkling his nose, Connor swept Taylor into his arms and began bouncing her, which quieted her for the moment.

"Man, that thing is foul! You've got to go after Anna and work something out."

"I tried every trick I know to 'work something out,' as you put it, when she was here. Nothing worked."

"Every trick but time. She wasn't here *that* long."

"Look, big, know-it-all, bossy-as-hell brother. You hired

me to find her. I found her. She ran off and kept my kid from me. I found her again. Now she's left again. Maybe for good. I think it's time I moved on with my life."

"She's confused."

"No. I think she wants a divorce. I think it's time I gave up on Anna Barton. Okay? Let's leave it at that."

"That's cruel."

"Sometimes, life's cruel and capricious. And so is love. And you know, sometimes there's not a damn thing we can do about those things even if we want to. So, maybe I don't like this situation of being a single dad all that much, but I'll get through it. When Linda died and then I found out she'd been pregnant, all I wanted was another chance. I thought Anna was that chance. I was wrong."

"What about Taylor?"

"She's everything to me now. I won't kid you, it tears me up when she starts crying and won't stop, and I know she wants Anna. But this is Anna's choice."

"Can I say one more thing?"

"As long as it's not about Anna and me."

"Terence says he's willing to try to help out with the baby until you can hire someone. Said he'll try his hand at baby-sitting. I'd make sure the kid's napping and doesn't need her diaper changed if I were you the first time he shows up."

Connor laughed. "Tell him anytime. I'm desperate."

Taylor laughed, too. Then she grabbed her daddy's nose and said, "Mamama…"

Holding Taylor, Connor pointed to the red bands of clouds streaking the blue sky that blazed above the tree tops in the strangely serene Houston sky.

A very bad-tempered storm named Janice had just whirled into the Gulf of Mexico and was heading straight for the Texas coast. Maybe for Houston.

"Clouds," he said, referring to the first storm bands that were a harbinger of far worse.

"Mamama," Taylor cried, patting his carved face trustingly with her soft, pink fingers.

"No, my little darling—*dadada*," he corrected. "Sorry to tell you, Hurricane Janice is going to be rattling our doors, not your pretty mama."

When he squeezed her tightly and kissed her loudly on her rounded belly, she touched his cheek again and giggled. For the first time since Anna had left them, she'd slept peacefully last night.

"We'll get there, baby girl," he whispered. "Together."

Even this late in the afternoon the air was so hot and ominous, he felt as if he were smothering. He hadn't yet decided whether to leave or to go. By the time it was clear what people should do it would be too late. Everybody in the damn city would hop in his car at the same time and jam the evacuation routes to the north. Connor wasn't sure he could handle twenty-four hours or more on the road alone with a baby to travel to a destination that normally took three. The nannies he'd hired had left this morning with their own families to avoid the traffic.

As he headed into his shadowy backyard, chainsaws roared high above him in his tall pine trees. He'd hired a two-man crew, and they were in harnesses cutting out the dead limbs so they wouldn't fall on the roof. His boots crunching into the pine needles and pinecones, he strode over to check on the men attaching his storm shutters. In the past he'd taken care of such tasks himself, but since the nannies had evacuated to Austin, Taylor was his top priority.

Fortunately, Janice was predicted to hit the coast a hundred miles to the south. Still, the jet stream and the first norther of the year just might push the storm to the north if it the hurricane sped up. And once in the open gulf, big storms frequently put the pedal to the metal.

Connor returned to his front yard just as a white Lincoln pulled over to the curb. Abby waved, got out in a flurry of blue skirts and sprinted up the lawn to them.

Knowing too well what she and the rest of Anna's family wanted, he frowned.

"You know I've hired people to find Anna again," she said.

"I told you. She's going to call. But it's your choice," he replied shortly.

"They've had no luck."

"Obviously she doesn't want to be found yet."

"I've come here to beg you to help us."

For a long moment they just stood there together, each of them looking at the thickening swirls of fire high in the sky instead of each other.

"Look," he said, "I'm sorry you lost your sister. I know how close you two used to be. She'll call you one day."

"I know." She brushed Taylor's soft cheek, and Taylor cooed flirtatiously. "Guess I'd better go," Abby said.

When Abby turned and headed to her car, Taylor fisted her chubby hands and cried, "Mamamama."

"You could have gone all night without doing that, baby

girl," he whispered. "You're just like your mama, aren't you, determined to tear my heart out."

In spite of himself, he smiled.

Carrollton, Georgia

Was there anything worse than to wake up at 2:00 a.m. from a nightmare in the middle of a stormy night alone, wanting your husband to hold you, only to realize your waking reality was worse than any nightmare?

In Anna's dream, something was chasing her through a dark, frightening forest. She'd heard crashing sounds right behind her.

Suddenly, she'd seen tall white walls, and a gate had opened. Only Connor, not Sister Kate, had been standing there with his arms held wide. He'd smiled his beautiful, welcoming smile.

She'd called to him, but his smile had died. And his darkly handsome face had dissolved into nothingness.

She ached to be in his arms, but she was all alone. Connor wasn't coming to save her ever again. And it was her fault.

The rain that slashed the windows of Anna's grubby studio apartment in Georgia had nothing to do with the hurricane pounding in faraway Texas, which she'd been tracking for days. Clutching her thin sheets to her throat, Anna sat up on her secondhand air mattress that had leaked air so badly she needed to blow it up again. She turned on the lamp beside her mattress and then her tiny TV. Bathed in a circle of golden light and comforted by the flickering pictures of the hurricane coverage on the Weather Channel, she felt marginally calmer.

If a relatively small storm could be this bad, she felt desperate to know what was happening to Taylor and Connor back in Texas.

She'd tried to call earlier, but Connor hadn't answered any of his phones. For the rest of the day she'd watched the Weather Channel in earnest. Hurricane Janice had screamed onto Galveston Island, destroying everything in its path, and was now barreling north-northwest toward Houston. She hadn't been able to learn all that much because the reporters riding out the storm were trapped and isolated themselves, and the same stock footage of parking lots and blowing palm trees looped endlessly.

Had her family felt like this when they'd lost her? Too late, she realized she didn't want a divorce. No matter how risky love was, being alone like this hurt more. No longer was she an independent, separate human being.

Maybe she'd had to get away to know how much Connor had become part of her. But before these thoughts and emotions had gelled, the hurricane had barreled into the Gulf.

Would Connor want her back? She didn't know. All she knew was that the thought of an empty future without him scared her a lot more than anything else ever had.

She wanted Connor's love and forgiveness. She wanted to be a mother and watch their child grow up together. If he would take her back, she would show him in a million ways how much she loved him every day for the rest of her life.

Mornings and afternoons when she looked after Mr. Janasak, who had Alzheimer's, she could hardly focus on her duties. He never remembered who she was or why she was there, but she was even more forgetful than he was. When he was slow or asked her the same question dozens of times, she felt angry and impatient because all she could think about was Connor and Taylor. Mr. Janasak deserved someone who could concentrate solely on him.

Now, not knowing if her family was safe made her realize that she couldn't live by herself another second.

A transformer blew, and her lamp, her tiny television and the streetlights outside went out. With a startled cry, she crawled across the darkened room to her purse. Shaking its contents onto the hardwood floor, she grabbed her cell phone and punched in Connor's Houston number again. When it rang and rang, her fingers tightened painfully.

Finally he answered. "This is Connor."

"Thank God," she whispered.

There was a lot of static. She heard something banging and a baby crying.

"Connor, is that Taylor? Is she okay?"

"She's all right." His voice was so cold, Anna knew he'd known her instantly.

"I miss her…so much."

"It's 2:00 a.m.," he said. "What the hell do you want? This is no time to discuss our divorce."

"Why is she crying?"

"I asked you what you wanted."

"Not a divorce. I was wrong…so wrong. I was watching the storm and feeling so far away from you and Taylor and everybody I love. I love you, Connor."

"For how long this time?"

"Forever."

"Right. And I'm supposed to believe you."

"Please—"

"Where the hell are you, anyway?"

"All I'm asking for is another chance."

"That's a helluva lot, sweetheart."

Glass shattered in the background. Taylor shrieked.

"What happened?" Anna screamed, feeling faint with terror.

"A tree, maybe. Water's pouring inside now." Connor cursed vividly. "It sounds like a train out there. Look, I gotta—" The line abruptly went dead.

She tried calling back, but got a message saying all the circuits were busy. Frantically, she called again and again—until her cell phone ran out of power. Then she just sat in the dark and prayed while the rain beat against her window and God-knew-what was happening to her husband and baby girl back in Texas.

All the signs on the Interstate between Georgia and Texas told motorists to stay clear of the Houston area. Radio newscasters warned that due to power outages and downed trees, nobody was being allowed in or out of Houston.

Anna had to find a way. She had to get to Connor and Taylor.

It was dark when she finally drove past Houston's city limits sign on I-10. She was exhausted. She'd driven over twenty-four hours straight, and since she couldn't reach Connor by phone, she was nervous about what she might find, as well.

She turned off the freeway onto the boulevard that led to Connor's neighborhood and saw a large officer and his police car blocking the road.

As her foot hit the brake, she frowned.

Biting her lip, she rolled her window down. The officer smiled and asked for her driver's license.

He barely glanced at it before handing it back to her. "I can't let you through. You're not from around here."

"But I am!" Anna replied.

His thick jaw hardening, he leaned down and peered into her Toyota. "Not according to your driver's license, you're not."

"That's because I used to live in Louisiana."

He was looking at her with cold, hard eyes.

She couldn't let him stop her. She had to get home to Connor.

"Really, I just live about a mile down this road. My little girl and husband will be scared to death if I don't show up."

He shook his head. "Sorry. We've got a curfew and orders not to let anyone into Houston. A tornado took out a house or two down that road. You'll have to turn around."

A tornado. "But I've driven day and night all the way from Georgia. You don't understand. I have to get back to my family. I've been gone a long time. Way too long."

"I didn't make this decision. The mayor did. The city doesn't have water or power or passable roads or even much gasoline. Just get back on the interstate."

"But my family needs me. And I need to know that they're all right. Please..."

"Sorry." Shaking his head, he stood up and motioned to the next car. There was nothing for her to do but to turn around.

Her white-knuckled hands spun the wheel obediently. She was halfway through the turn, when the big cop leaned inside the next car.

Like hell she'd turn around!

She didn't really think. She just spun the wheel in the opposite direction and hit the gas.

Fortunately, the big cop was too busy to do more than holler. Not that she got very far. Half a mile from Connor's house, a downed pine lay across the road. She slammed on the brakes. Without bothering to remove the keys, she got out and climbed over the pine and ran the rest of the way.

It was dark, and since no streetlights or houselights were on anywhere, Connor's large home loomed threateningly out of a sea of broken tree limbs. But at least it was still intact.

As she looked closer, she saw that its shutters were closed, and that the brown waters of the bayou encroached on the lawn. A huge pine had fallen on one corner of the garage and had smashed a window, but the main part of the house looked intact.

Picking her way through limbs and debris while watching for snakes, she cleared a path to his front door.

Lifting a slim hand, she rapped timidly with her knuckles. When he didn't answer, she banged with both fists. "Connor!"

She was about to give up when the door cracked half an inch.

"Connor?" She barely dared to breathe.

At the sight of her through that slit, Connor's unsmiling face became so blank and hard, she felt a swift rush of hot color flood her neck and face.

"I had to know if you and Taylor made it."

"Well, now you know."

She stood her ground.

"I said we're fine." His brows snapped together. His

mouth thinned when she still didn't move. "Damn you to hell and back! We're fine!"

"Please…I drove all night. I…I don't want a divorce!"

His wild blue eyes pierced her. "Why should I give a damn?"

"Please, Connor, you have to at least listen to me."

"No. I don't have to do anything. Not anymore." He looked so furious, he probably would have slammed the door in her face if she hadn't slipped her foot inside.

"I'm not leaving," she said. "Not till we talk. I'll…I'll crawl. I'll beg." Her eyes stung hotly. "Connor, I'm so tired. Please let me in. I haven't eaten since Georgia. I feel like if I don't sit down soon, I'll probably fall down." She dabbed at her damp eyes with heartfelt emotion.

His angry gaze drilled into her for so long, she couldn't believe it when he opened the door and stood back. "What do you want?" he said.

"I told you. You. Taylor. Forever."

"Right." He caught her to him and tilted her chin up so he could stare directly into her eyes. His soul-searching stare made her feel incredibly vulnerable even as it made her see how naked and raw his own emotions really were.

"Don't say that if you don't mean it," he said. "I can't take much more."

"I swear I'll never leave you again."

"What if you get scared or want to be on your own?"

"I think I've changed. I want you and Taylor and the rest of my family more than anything. I was way more terrified alone in Georgia, worrying about you and Taylor and everybody else when I didn't know what was happening to all of you."

"Like your twin sister and father were, worrying about you all those years."

"Yes. And I've thought about them a lot. I want to get to know them. I can't live without any of you."

"It took you a while to come to that conclusion."

"I put myself in hell. I have no one to blame but me. Please…please give me another chance."

He smiled. Then slowly, carefully, he wrapped her in his arms. "No, sweetheart, those bad guys put you in hell. Welcome back."

"Most of all I want to be your wife," she said, laying her head against the solid warmth of his chest.

"You already are. You're everything…simply everything to me. And maybe you have been from the first moment I saw you. Hey, I wasn't perfect, either. So, I'm not going to harp on the fact that you put me through hell this past month. Taylor, too. I had to learn about babies pretty fast, wean Taylor from breast milk to the bottle, hire a nanny. Two, in fact. Taylor's been pretty grumpy."

"I'll spend the rest of my life trying to make that up to both of you. You saved me and gave me enough confidence and love to start fighting for what I really want. I want us to be a family."

"I guess all that matters is that you've finally found the courage to stop running."

He began to kiss her, and soon they both wanted only one thing—to be together. But first, carrying a candle through the dark house, they checked on Taylor. Since she was asleep Anna had to be content with kissing her velvet-soft brow. Then Connor led her down the floating stairs to their magical bedroom.

He lay down on the bed, and she began to strip by the light of that single candle, shedding her T-shirt and jeans slowly.

"I saved a bathtub full of water before the storm hit," he said, watching her breasts that were lit up with flickering gold. "So we can wash up, before and after."

"Later," she said softly. "It's been too long."

"Same here," he rasped, his voice full of hunger.

She lay down beside him and curled her body against the warm, solid length of his. As always she fit perfectly. On a groan he pulled her against him, touched his lips to her throat and then to each of her breasts. With a sigh, she raised her arms and stretched.

She felt safe. So blissfully safe. And so loved, even before he began to make love to her.

The frightened little girl who'd been kidnapped at eight and had been on her own ever since had come home at last.

Then Connor was kissing Anna in earnest, and she was kissing him with equal abandon. She held her breath when he sat up and blew the candle out. Wrapping her in his arms again, he kissed her deeply.

She felt safe, cherished, adored.

This is forever, she thought. Happily ever after. Forever.

"I love you," she whispered.

"Show me."

She laughed. "With pleasure."

Slowly she lowered her head and began kissing him everywhere.

"Your turn," she begged.

He began by kissing her brow, then her cheeks and, last of all, her lips.

"That's how we'll do it, you know. We'll erase the bad

memories by building beautiful memories until one day you'll have so many beautiful memories, there won't be any shadows."

He caught her chin with gentle fingers and held it still before lowering his mouth to hers again. "Sorry, I didn't expect this. Do you want me to shave?"

"No."

Except for the roughness of his chin, his kisses were sweet and tender, but she didn't want gentleness. Digging her fingers into his broad shoulders, her ravenous mouth devoured his until she had him shuddering against her lips, his pleasure as fierce as hers.

She licked his nipples and then his belly button. Raising her head again, she kissed his lips. He aligned himself over her. At her breathless urging, he gasped and then eased himself inside her. Their bodies fused, he held her close for a long moment. She kissed the tip of his nose, savoring this special time of soul-deep togetherness before their passion took over and they lost control.

"Connor, I love you," she whispered.

He kissed her mouth in response. Then his body pressed close and his hands dug into her shoulders.

She arched upward, urging him to thrust deeper.

"Take me," she begged. "I'm burning up. I can't think. *Please!* Now!"

He groaned. "You're so damn beautiful. God, I missed you. So much."

His lips moved over her face, down her neck to her breasts. Each whispery kiss rasped across her soft skin, flooding her with molten warmth. She opened herself to him completely, knowing that even as she moved against him, enticing him with her mouth and hands and hips to go faster and harder, he was still holding back.

"Connor," she urged, sliding against him.

His grip around her waist tightened. Then he could restrain himself no longer. Straddling her, he plunged wildly again and again. She wrapped her legs around him, hugging him tightly.

Never before had she given herself so completely, both emotionally and physically. Higher and higher they soared, riding each other, exploding, crying out. Breathing hard, they laughed when their bodies finally stilled.

He pulled her close. "We're going to be happy. So happy. I swear."

Softly, she threaded her fingers through his hair. Then she nuzzled his warm skin so she could inhale his clean, male scent. She ran her hand over his back, narrow waist and beautiful, sculpted legs, marveling at how gorgeous he was.

"Anna," he breathed. "Oh, Anna."

"Becky," she corrected. "You can call me Becky."

"Promise you won't run away when I do?"

She laughed. "Never again. I promise. I've come home to stay."

"Becky," he murmured, infinite love in his low tone.

The name felt good, so good and true. So right.

She couldn't wait to see the rest of her family—Abby, Terence, Caesar, Leo and all the Kembles. But not tonight.

Tonight was for Connor.

Epilogue

The Golden Spurs Ranch
Labor Day Weekend

The dinner bell rang just as the last rays of the setting sun swept across the pasture, lighting the spurs in the ancient mesquite's spindly branches.

This particular mesquite tree was more than a pesky mesquite tree. The Spur Tree held a legendary significance to the small band of family members grouped around it.

"Time for dinner," a woman's voice yelled impatiently from the Big House.

The dinner on the veranda and in the tents set up behind the Big House was being held in honor of Becky's return. All the ranchers from the nearby counties had been invited. Dozens of friends from San Antonio and

Austin had flown down for the party. Even the governor was coming.

The ranch's long-lost princess was home at last.

"Time for dinner," the woman shouted a second time.

"That would be Sy'rai," Leo said. "If we're smart, we'd better get back to the house before she loses her temper. She doesn't like her food to get cold."

Becky's hand closed around the pair of spurs Lizzy, her older half sister, had just handed her. "Well, thank you for these."

"You're home again, so they don't belong on the tree anymore," Lizzy said in a soft voice.

"Then I'll keep them in a safe place," Becky murmured.

"The Spur Tree probably doesn't seem like much to look at, at least not to most folks," Lizzy continued.

"Because they don't know its legendary history," Connor said.

"Some would call it a morbid history," Leo countered.

"Those of us with an irreverent nature." Connor grinned. "A lot of people have made a lot of sacrifices to build this ranch into what it is today. Some of us respect that." Having removed his Stetson, he held it against his heart, his expression that of a man who believed he was standing near something sacred. That, however, didn't stop him from sneakily kicking a pebble toward his brother's boot or squeezing Becky's hand possessively.

"Whenever a man or woman who belongs to this ranch or has contributed to it leaves for any time at all, we hang their spurs here till they come back," Lizzy said.

"And you've come back," Joanne said to Becky, even as she glanced toward Terence.

"At last," Connor whispered.

"Forever," Becky whispered back to him.

Terence, who stood beside Joanne, had his arm wrapped loosely around her waist. They'd been a couple ever since Becky had come home. Becky was glad her father had found somebody, and she knew that if she hadn't come home, he'd probably be living in some awful jungle risking death.

Every day that she was with these people, especially Connor, she felt stronger and braver and happier.

Suddenly Connor turned and pulled her close. She felt a buzz of excitement as his warm lips touched the corner of her mouth.

"I love you," he whispered in that warm tone he used only with her. "I love you."

Her family was watching them while pretending not to, and everybody was smiling.

She felt loved by one and all. And safe. And oh so happy.

* * * * *

*Celebrate 60 years of pure reading pleasure
with Harlequin®!*

*Harlequin Presents® is proud to introduce
its gripping new miniseries,*
THE ROYAL HOUSE OF KAREDES.
*An exquisite coronation diamond, split as a symbol
of a warring royal family's feud, is missing!
But whoever reunites the diamond halves
will rule all....*

*Welcome to eight brand-new titles that unfold
to reveal the stories of kings and queens, princes and
princesses torn apart by pride and power, but finally
reunited by love.*

Step into the world of Karedes with
*BILLIONAIRE PRINCE, PREGNANT MISTRESS
Available July 2009 from Harlequin Presents®.*

ALEXANDROS KAREDES, SNOW DUSTING the shoulders of his leather jacket and glittering like jewels in his dark hair, stood at the door. Maria felt the blood drain from her head.

"Good evening, Ms. Santos."

His voice was as she remembered it. Deep. Husky. Perfect English, but with the faintest hint of a Greek accent. And cold, as cold as it had been that awful morning she would never forget, when he'd accused her of horrible things, called her terrible names....

"Aren't you going to ask me in?"

She fought for composure. Last time they'd faced each other, they'd been on his turf. Now they were on hers. She was in command here, and that meant everything.

"There's a sign on the door downstairs," she said, her tone every bit as frigid as his. "It says, 'No soliciting or vagrants.'"

His lips drew back in a wolfish grin. "Very amusing."

"What do you want, Prince Alexandros?"

A tight smile eased across his mouth and it killed her that even now, knowing he was a vicious, arrogant man, she couldn't help but notice what a handsome mouth it was. Chiseled. Generous. Beautiful, like the rest of him, which made him living proof that beauty could, indeed, be only skin deep.

"Such formality, Maria. You were hardly so proper the last time we were together."

She knew his choice of words was deliberate. She felt her face heat; she couldn't help that but she damned well didn't have to let him lure her into a verbal sparring match.

"I'll ask you once more, Your Highness. What do you want?"

"Ask me in and I'll tell you."

"I have no intention of asking you in. Tell me why you're here or don't. It's your choice, just as it will be my choice to shut the door in your face."

He laughed. It infuriated her but she could hardly blame him. He was tall—six-two, six-three—and though he stood with one shoulder leaning against the door frame, hands tucked casually into the pockets of the jacket, his pose was deceptive. He was strong, with the leanly muscled body of a well-trained athlete.

She remembered his body with painful clarity. The feel of him under her hands. The power of him moving over her. The taste of him on her tongue.

Suddenly, he straightened, his laughter gone. "I have not come this distance to stand in your doorway," he said coldly, "and I am not going to leave until I am ready to do so. I suggest you stand aside and stop behaving like a petulant child."

A petulant child? Was that what he thought? This man who had spent hours making love to her and had then accused her of—of trading her body for profit?

Except it had not been love, it had been sex. And the sooner she got rid of him, the better.

She let go of the doorknob and stepped aside. "You have five minutes."

He strolled past her, bringing cold air and the scent of the night with him. She swung toward him, arms folded. He reached past her, pushed the door closed, then folded his arms, too. She wanted to open the door again but she'd be damned if she was going to get into a who's-in-charge-here argument with him. She was in charge, and he would surely see a tussle over the ground rules as a sign of weakness.

Instead, she looked past him at the big clock above her work table.

"Ten seconds gone," she said briskly. "You're wasting time, Your Highness."

"What I have to say will take longer than five minutes."

"Then you'll just have to learn to economize. More than five minutes, I'll call the police."

Instantly, his hand was wrapped around her wrist. He tugged her toward him, his dark-chocolate eyes almost black with anger.

"You do that and I'll tell every tabloid shark I can contact about how Maria Santos tried to buy a five-hundred-thousand-dollar commission by seducing a prince." He smiled thinly. "They'll lap it up."

What will it take for this billionaire prince
to realize he's falling in love with his mistress...?
Look for
BILLIONAIRE PRINCE, PREGNANT MISTRESS
by Sandra Marton
Available July 2009 from Harlequin Presents®.

Copyright © 2009 by Sandra Myles

We'll be spotlighting a different series every month
throughout 2009 to celebrate our 60th anniversary.

Look for Harlequin® Presents in July!

TWO CROWNS, TWO ISLANDS, ONE LEGACY
A royal family, torn apart by pride and its lust for
power, reunited by purity and passion

Step into the world of Karedes
beginning this July with

BILLIONAIRE PRINCE, PREGNANT MISTRESS
by

Sandra Marton

Eight volumes to collect and treasure!

www.eHarlequin.com   HPBPA09

You're invited to join our Tell Harlequin Reader Panel!

By joining our new reader panel you will:

- Receive Harlequin® books—they are FREE and yours to keep with no obligation to purchase anything!
- Participate in fun online surveys
- Exchange opinions and ideas with women just like you
- Have a say in our new book ideas and help us publish the best in women's fiction

In addition, you will have a chance to win great prizes and receive special gifts! See Web site for details. Some conditions apply. Space is limited.

To join, visit us at
www.TellHarlequin.com.

THBPA0108

What's a STEELE to do when he comes home to find a beautiful woman asleep in his bed?

NEW YORK TIMES BESTSELLING AUTHOR

BRENDA JACKSON

Playboy Donovan Steele has one goal: to make sultry Natalie Ford his latest conquest. She's resisting, but their sizzling chemistry makes her think twice. Once she reveals her true identity, will Donovan disappear—for good?

On sale JUNE 30, 2009
wherever books are sold.

Indulge in the latest Forged of Steele novel, the anticipated follow-up to IRRESISTIBLE FORCES.

KIMANI™ ROMANCE

www.kimanipress.com
www.myspace.com/kimanipress

KPBJI20SP

HQN™

We *are* romance™

New York Times bestselling author

Susan Andersen

turns up the heat in this classic tale of old flames igniting a new spark....

When Victoria Hamilton's vacation fling resulted in a baby, she began a new life far from her family's corrupting influence. But when her half brother becomes the prime suspect in a murder case, she returns home—coming face-to-face with her old fling....And private investigator John "Rocket" Miglionni sure isn't about to let the woman of his dreams get away a second time!

Hot & Bothered

Available now wherever books are sold!

www.HQNBooks.com

PHSA419

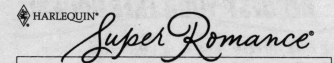

THE BELLES OF TEXAS

They're as strong as the state that raised them. The Belle sisters aren't afraid to go after what they want, whether it's reclaiming their ranch or their family.

Linda Warren
CAITLYN'S PRIZE

Thanks to her deceased father's gambling debts, Caitlyn Belle's beloved High Five Ranch is in dire straits. Particularly because the will stipulates that if the ranch doesn't turn a profit in six months, it must be sold to Judd Calhoun—the man Caitlyn jilted fourteen years ago. And Cait knows Judd has been waiting a long time for his revenge....

*Look for the first book
in The Belles of Texas miniseries,
on sale in July wherever books are sold.*

REQUEST YOUR FREE BOOKS!

2 FREE NOVELS PLUS 2 FREE GIFTS!

Silhouette®

Desire®

Passionate, Powerful, Provocative!

YES! Please send me 2 FREE Silhouette Desire® novels and my 2 FREE gifts (gifts are worth about $10). After receiving them, if I don't wish to receive any more books, I can return the shipping statement marked "cancel". If I don't cancel, I will receive 6 brand-new novels every month and be billed just $4.05 per book in the U.S. or $4.74 per book in Canada. That's a savings of almost 15% off the cover price! It's quite a bargain! Shipping and handling is just 50¢ per book.* I understand that accepting the 2 free books and gifts places me under no obligation to buy anything. I can always return a shipment and cancel at any time. Even if I never buy another book, the two free books and gifts are mine to keep forever.   225 SDN EYMS 326 SDN EYM4

Name   (PLEASE PRINT)

Address   Apt. #

City   State/Prov.   Zip/Postal Code

Signature (if under 18, a parent or guardian must sign)

Mail to the Silhouette Reader Service:
IN U.S.A.: P.O. Box 1867, Buffalo, NY 14240-1867
IN CANADA: P.O. Box 609, Fort Erie, Ontario L2A 5X3

Not valid to current subscribers of Silhouette Desire books.

**Want to try two free books from another line?
Call 1-800-873-8635 or visit www.morefreebooks.com.**

* Terms and prices subject to change without notice. Prices do not include applicable taxes. Sales tax applicable in N.Y. Canadian residents will be charged applicable provincial taxes and GST. Offer not valid in Quebec. This offer is limited to one order per household. All orders subject to approval. Credit or debit balances in a customer's account(s) may be offset by any other outstanding balance owed by or to the customer. Please allow 4 to 6 weeks for delivery. Offer available while quantities last.

Your Privacy: Silhouette Books is committed to protecting your privacy. Our Privacy Policy is available online at www.eHarlequin.com or upon request from the Reader Service. From time to time we make our lists of customers available to reputable third parties who may have a product or service of interest to you. If you would prefer we not share your name and address, please check here. ☐

SDES09R

In 2009 Harlequin celebrates
60 years of pure reading pleasure!

We're marking this occasion by offering
16 **FREE** full books to download and read.

Visit

www.HarlequinCelebrates.com

to choose from a variety of
great romance stories
that are absolutely **FREE!**

(Total approximate retail value of $60)

We invite you to visit and share the Web site
with your friends, family
and anyone who enjoys reading.

SMP60WEB1

Silhouette Desire

COMING NEXT MONTH
Available July 14, 2009

#1951 ROYAL SEDUCER—Michelle Celmer
Man of the Month
The prince thought his bride-to-be knew their marriage was only a diplomatic arrangement. But their passion in the bedroom tells a different story….

#1952 TAMING THE TEXAS TYCOON—
Katherine Garbera
Texas Cattleman's Club: Maverick County Millionaires
Seducing his secretary wasn't part of the plan—yet now he'll never be satisfied with just one night.

#1953 INHERITED: ONE CHILD—Day Leclaire
Billionaires and Babies
Forced to marry to keep his niece, this billionaire finds the perfect solution in his very attractive nanny…until a secret she's harboring threatens to destroy everything.

#1954 THE ILLEGITIMATE KING—Olivia Gates
The Castaldini Crown
This potential heir will only take the crown on one condition—he'll take the king's daughter with it!

#1955 MAGNATE'S MAKE-BELIEVE MISTRESS—
Bronwyn Jameson
Secretly determined to expose his housekeeper's lies, he makes her his mistress to keep her close. But little does he know that he has the wrong sister!

#1956 HAVING THE BILLIONAIRE'S BABY—
Sandra Hyatt
After one hot night with his sister's enemy, he's stunned when she reveals she's carrying his baby!

SDCNMBPA0609